Ivy's mouth was downturned at the corners, her shoulders slumped.

"I'm still a virgin and I'm almost thirty. I need to do something to fix myself otherwise I'll never find a partner, especially today when everyone's so adventurous and open about sex. I'm a pariah. An uptight prude who can't even get undressed unless the lights are out."

To say Louis was shocked was an understatement. Almost thirty and still a virgin? Louis put his glass of whiskey down and took a deep steadying breath. "Firstly, Ivy, you don't have to fix anything. You should only do what you're comfortable doing when and only when you're comfortable doing it."

"But I might never be comfortable if I don't do something sooner rather than later. I can't go on like this. It's beyond embarrassing going on a date with a new guy and then bolting out the door as soon as he touches me."

Louis rapidly blinked. Tried to ignore the little stab of unease in his gut about her hooking up with some guy she barely knew. "Let me get this straight... You want me to sleep with you?"

Melanie Milburne

ONE NIGHT ON THE VIRGIN'S TERMS

HARLEQUIN®
PRESENTS®

Recycling programs
for this product may
not exist in your area.

ISBN-13: 978-1-335-14885-8

One Night on the Virgin's Terms

Copyright © 2020 by Melanie Milburne

This edition published by arrangement with Harlequin Books S.A.

For questions and comments about the quality of this book,
please contact us at CustomerService@Harlequin.com.

Harlequin Enterprises ULC
22 Adelaide St. West, 40th Floor
Toronto, Ontario M5H 4E3, Canada
www.Harlequin.com

Printed in U.S.A.

Melanie Milburne read her first Harlequin novel at the age of seventeen, in between studying for her final exams. After completing a master's degree in education, she decided to write a novel, and thus her career as a romance author was born. Melanie is an ambassador for the Australian Childhood Foundation and a keen dog lover and trainer. She enjoys long walks in the Tasmanian bush. In 2015 Melanie won the HOLT Medallion, a prestigious award honoring outstanding literary talent.

Books by Melanie Milburne

Harlequin Presents

A Virgin for a Vow
Blackmailed into the Marriage Bed
Tycoon's Forbidden Cinderella
The Return of Her Billionaire Husband

Conveniently Wed!

Bound by a One-Night Vow
Penniless Virgin to Sicilian's Bride
Billionaire's Wife on Paper

Once Upon a Temptation

His Innocent's Passionate Awakening

Secret Heirs of Billionaires

Cinderella's Scandalous Secret

The Scandal Before the Wedding

Claimed for the Billionaire's Convenience
The Venetian One-Night Baby

Visit the Author Profile page
at Harlequin.com for more titles.

To my editor and shadow editor Nic Caws and Hannah Rossiter. Thank you both for being so supportive through my at times (more times than I'd like!) difficult writing process. Your faith and confidence in me is so appreciated. Bless you!

xxxx

CHAPTER ONE

Ivy Kennedy was at the hairdresser's when she found a solution to her virginity problem. The answer was in the very first gossip magazine she flicked through. Truth be told, the answer had been under her nose for years, but it hadn't been until now that she'd had her *Aha!* moment.

Louis Charpentier—the king of one-night stands and her older brother's best friend. Her problem solved. Who knew that getting highlights could be the highlight of your week? Your month? Your year?

Sarina, the hairstylist, glanced over Ivy's shoulder at the magazine article and whistled through her teeth. 'Gosh, isn't Louis Charpentier enough to stop your heart? I swear that man should come with a warning. He's so gorgeous, I'm getting a hot flash just looking at his photo. I hear he's won Hottest Bachelor of the Year again. How many times is that now? Three?'

'Four.'

Ivy turned the page over but surreptitiously used her left thumb as a bookmark. She wanted another look at Louis without the hairdresser drooling over her shoulder.

She gave what she hoped would pass as an indifferent shrug and added, 'He's okay, I guess.'

For years Louis had been nothing more than her brother Ronan's best friend. Handsome enough, but not enough to 'tempt her', to borrow a phrase from Jane Austen. But, with her thirtieth birthday rapidly approaching, and her status as a virgin unchanged, she had to do something—and soon.

How was she ever going to find a partner in life unless she did something about her embarrassing intimacy issues? She'd spent most of her adult life finding any excuse she could to avoid dating, out of fear. Fear of being naked with a man and him finding her not good enough. Fear of being hurt. Fear of falling in love with someone only for them to dump her.

But she was about to turn thirty, and she had to push past this road block in her life. Thirty. *Eek!* Who'd ever heard of a thirty-year-old virgin these days?

And who better to fix her little problem than Louis, who was super-experienced at seduction. How could her inhibitions around sex be solved any other way? It would be awkward and cringe-worthy, asking him, but she couldn't bear the thought of asking anyone else.

She wanted someone she knew and trusted to help her, not some casual hook-up who might laugh at her or mock her for still being a virgin at her age. Or make rude comments about her body, like one of her erstwhile dates. Louis wasn't a stranger, he was a friend… Well, perhaps a 'friend', inverted commas, would be more accurate.

Now that her brother had emigrated to Australia to be with his partner Ricky, Ivy only saw Louis for a coffee or lunch now and again. And she'd had to cancel the last time due to a large shipment of antiques arriving from France at the store where she worked as a curator.

Ivy knew that if she didn't act on her decision this very afternoon she might lose her courage and not act at all. She only had a month until she turned the big Three O, but she wanted to experience the Big O well before then. The birthday clock was ticking like a bomb.

She took a deep breath, opened the magazine again and studied Louis' distinctive features. Tall and dark, with his smoky blue-grey gaze brooding in an I-don't-quite-know-what-he's-thinking kind of way, he was the epitome of heart-stopping gorgeousness. She traced the firm line of his mouth in the photo and began to imagine how it would feel pressed to her own. Her eyes went further down the photo to his strongly muscled thighs and a soft flutter of nerves wafted through her belly.

She closed the magazine with a definitive snap. Yep. He was The One. Not as in a happily-ever-after The One, but the perfect solution to her embarrassing problem.

All she had to do was convince him.

Louis Charpentier was doing the final drafts of a major architectural project in his London office when his secretary buzzed him on the intercom.

'Louis? There's—' she began.

'I said no interruptions this afternoon, Maureen.' He injected his tone with stern authority. Why couldn't his temporary secretary obey his simple instructions, for God's sake? He was on a tight deadline and the client was difficult and demanding. Story of his life. What was it about him that attracted the most demanding clients? No doubt the same bad-luck fairy that had given him difficult and demanding parents.

'I'm sorry, but there's a Miss Ivy Kennedy here to see you. She hasn't made an appointment but she insists it's important she sees you as soon as possible. She says she's the sister of a close friend of yours. Will I send her in or tell her to come back some other time?'

Louis pushed his computer mouse to one side and scraped a hand through his hair. What could be wrong? Ivy had cancelled the last time he'd suggested they have lunch. Her brother Ronan had asked him to keep an eye on her when he'd emigrated to Australia. Louis enjoyed his occasional catch-ups with Ivy, but he tried not to notice her in any way that could be even loosely described as sexual. Not easy to do when she looked so damn sexy without even trying. But messing with his best mate's kid sister was a no-go zone. Ivy was the hanging out for the fairy tale, the forever love. She was the wanting-to-have-babies type. He was the sleep-with-them-once-and-move-on-without-looking-back type. They had zilch in common other than her brother Ronan. Besides, his best mate had experienced enough trouble coming out to his family without Louis adding more to the mix.

Louis pressed the button on the intercom. 'Send her in. And hold all my calls until she leaves. Understood?'

'Got it.'

The door opened and Louis rose from behind his desk, his eyes scanning the pint-sized whirlwind that came in. With almost waist-length wavy red-gold hair, periwinkle-blue eyes, Celtic alabaster skin and a full-lipped mouth, Ivy Kennedy looked as if she had stepped out of another era—apart from her clothes, of course. He tried not to stare too long at her slim legs encased in blindingly white jeans, and the way her black V-neck cashmere sweater outlined the firm up-thrust of her small but perfect breasts. She was wearing burgundy heeled, pointy-toed ankle boots that highlighted the daintiness of her ankles. But even with the boost of her heels she still didn't make it up to his shoulder.

'Hello Ivy.' His voice came out a little huskier than he'd intended, and he was conscious of the effort it took to keep his gaze away from the ripe, plump curve of her mouth. 'What can I do for you?'

'Louis, I hope you don't mind me coming to see you like this, but I have a problem and I think you're the only one who can help me.' Her voice was breathless and twin circles of colour formed on her cheeks.

Louis was never sure whether to greet her with a kiss on the cheek or a hug but, given the way his groin was stirring just now, a hug was very definitely out.

Maybe his self-imposed celibacy was a mistake. Mr Amazing One-Night Stand was taking a much-needed sabbatical. How long had it been? Three, or was it four, months? He stayed behind his desk and waved a hand to the chair in front of the desk reserved for clients. 'Please, sit down.'

'Thanks. I won't take up too much of your time.' Ivy plonked herself down on the chair, her dangling silver costume-earrings swaying against her heart-shaped face. He caught a whiff of her perfume—white lilacs and lily-of-the-valley—which danced around his nostrils in an intoxicating vapor. Her small, neat hands were clasped around a rectangular bag only big enough to carry a mobile phone and the bare essentials. She ran the tip of her tongue across her cherry-red lips and then gave him a dimpled smile that almost knocked him off his feet. Small white teeth with an adorable overbite and those luscious lips were a bewitching combination that sent his pulse up another notch. 'It's good to see you, Louis. Sorry I had to take a rain check last time.'

Stop staring at her mouth. And don't even think about looking at her breasts.

'That's okay. I had a lot on that week anyway.' He cleared his throat and sat down, resting his forearms on the desk. 'So, what can I help you with?' He used his let's-get-down-to-business tone, but he was aware of a strange energy in the air—a subtle tightening of the atmosphere that made the black hairs on his arms tingle at the roots.

She rolled her lips together, her gaze lowering to the Windsor knot of his tie as if she found it the most fascinating thing in the world. 'Erm... Well, it's kind of difficult to explain...' Her cheeks went two shades darker and her fingers picked at the stitching on her bag as if she was determined to dismantle it then and there. He automatically checked her left hand for rings. Nothing.

He let go of a breath he hadn't realised he'd been holding. He lived in silent dread of her getting involved with the wrong man. It would be just his luck to have her fall for some totally unsuitable guy on his watch. Her brother had told him she'd been dreaming about getting married since she'd been given her first doll. He'd also heard she'd been unlucky in the dating game, no doubt because she was way too generous and trusting and not at all street-smart.

Louis leaned back in his chair and reached up to loosen the knot of his tie. 'Would you like a drink? Coffee? Tea? Something stronger?'

Ivy glanced at him, her small white teeth snagging her bottom lip. 'Do you have any brandy?'

He frowned. 'Since when do you drink brandy? I thought you only drank white wine or champagne.'

Her lips twitched in a self-deprecating smile, her cute dimples appearing. 'This is kind of a brandy situation.'

'Now you've got me intrigued.' Louis rose from his chair, walked over to his drinks cabinet and poured a small measure of brandy into a tumbler. He came over to where she was sitting and handed the brandy to her. Her fingers brushed his in the exchange and a current of electricity shot from her fingers to his and straight to his groin with lightning-bolt speed. What was going on with him today? He was acting like a hormone-mad teenager. Maybe his sex sabbatical wasn't such a great idea. It was messing with his head, messing with his morals, messing with his boundaries.

Louis perched on the corner of his desk in front of her chair rather than go back behind his desk. He told himself it would make her feel more at ease, less intimidated without the barrier of his huge desk between them, but deep down he knew it had more to do with wanting to be close enough to study every nuance of her face. He watched her lips move against the rim of the crystal tumbler, imagined them closing around him and a wave of heat swept through his body.

Yep, he really needed to break his sex drought. Getting the hots for his best friend's sister would be crossing a line he had sworn he would never cross. Ronan had issued him with the task of keeping an eye on her. Nothing else. Eyes on. Hands off. What else could there be between them? He wasn't her type in any shape or form. Ivy was the sweet, homespun type who couldn't walk past a jewellery-shop window without gazing at diamond engagement rings and wedding rings. The type of woman who tried on wedding dresses in her lunch hour. The type of woman who drooled over prams and puppies and dreamed of promises of forever love. He had no faith in that kind of love. How could he when he had watched his parents' forever love turn into forever fighting over the years?

Ivy took three eye-watering sips, coughed twice

and then leaned forward to put the glass on Louis' desk with a grimace. 'Gosh, how do people drink this stuff? I'm not sure I can finish it.'

'Probably a good thing.'

She hunted up her sleeve for a tissue and, taking one out, mopped at her eyes, giving him a sheepish look from beneath eyelashes as long and spiky as spiders' legs. 'I'm sorry for interrupting you when you're so busy. Is that a new secretary? She seems awfully nice.'

It was typical of Ivy to see the best in everybody. It was an endearing quality but not one he possessed. Maybe he was more like his father than he realised. *Shoot me now.* 'Yes, she's only been here a couple of months. My usual secretary, Natalie, is on maternity leave.'

Ivy leaned forward in a conspiratorial manner and continued in a stage whisper. 'I think she's a little bit in love with you.'

Louis coughed out a laugh and pushed himself off the desk with his hands. Maybe it wasn't such a good idea to sit so close to her. Her perfume was doing strange things to his senses—not to mention the glimpse he got of her delightful cleavage when she leaned forward. He moved back around behind his desk, sat on the chair and crossed one ankle over his bent knee in a casual pose he was far from feeling.

'I never mix business with pleasure, and dating

staff is a recipe for disaster.' Dating anyone for longer than twenty-four hours these days was a disaster. He'd once been fine with a week or two with someone, even a month, but that was before his most recent lover, who'd had trouble accepting the end of their three-week fling. Being stalked for weeks on end by a woman who'd fancied herself madly in love with him had been no fun. His new rule was one night and one night only. It gave no time for feelings to develop on either side.

Ivy rolled her lips together, her eyes briefly dipping to his mouth. 'Are you…seeing anyone at the moment?' Her voice had a tentative, breathless quality to it and the pink in her cheeks darkened.

Louis swivelled his chair in slow sideways movements, his gaze holding hers. 'Not at the moment. Why?'

She gave a one-shoulder shrug, her eyes skittering away from his. 'Just asking…'

He lowered his crossed ankle to the floor and leaned his arms on the desk again. 'Ivy.' He used his parent-to-child tone, because right then he was having way too much trouble seeing her as his mate's sister. He was seeing her naked in his bed, those gorgeous breasts in his hands, his mouth on hers, his…

Stop. Do not go any further. Just stop.

Ivy slow-blinked like a little owl. 'Can I ask you something?'

Louis sat back again and rubbed a hand over his late-in-the-day stubble. 'Yeah, sure. Go for it.'

She gave an audible swallow, the tip of her tongue sneaking out to deposit a layer of moisture on her lips. Lips he couldn't stop thinking about kissing, to see if they were as soft and pliable as they looked. To see what they tasted like—sweet or salty or a sexy combination of the two? 'Louis…what do you find most attractive in a woman? I mean, you date a lot, so I guess you'd know what's hot and what's not, right?'

What was hot was sitting right in front of him, with her small white teeth pulling at her lower lip. What was hot was thinking about peeling those skin-tight jeans and sweater off her and planting kisses on every inch of her body. What was hot was thinking about her legs wrapped around his hips while he drove them both to oblivion.

Louis suppressed a shudder and gave himself a vigorous mental shake. Anyone would think he was the one who'd drunk that brandy. 'Confidence is enormously attractive in a woman.'

Ivy slapped one of her thighs and sprang to her feet; her bag dropped to the floor with a thud but she didn't even seem to notice. 'I *knew* it. That's exactly what I think and it's why I'm here to ask for your help to gain some.'

Louis raised his brows a fraction. 'Me?'

She came around to his side of the desk, standing

close enough for him to touch her. *Do. Not. Touch. Her.* The temptation to do so was painfully difficult to resist. Her hair was a red-gold cloud around her neck and shoulders, and every time she moved her head he could smell the fruity fragrance of her shampoo. Her eyes were so bright they could have auditioned for a position in the Milky Way. And her lips… Dear God, her lips were plump and shimmering with lip-gloss, and it was all he could do not to lean forward and kiss her.

'Yes. You,' Ivy said, her smile triggering those cute dimples again. 'I wouldn't feel comfortable with anyone else. I need someone I know and trust. It would be too hard for me to do this with a stranger.'

Do what with a stranger? And why did she trust *him*? Louis wasn't so sure he deserved her trust, given where his mind was leading him—straight into the gutter. He pushed his chair back and stood, putting a little more distance between them. He went over to the drinks cabinet and poured himself a neat whisky. He wasn't a heavy drinker—thankfully that was one way in which he was different from his father—but right then he could have drained the bottle and followed it with a brandy chaser.

He took a measured sip and turned back to face her. 'I'm not sure I'm following you. What exactly do you want me to do?'

Ivy shifted from foot to foot, her hands interlaced

in front of her body, her cheeks blooming again with colour. 'I have a problem with…with sex…'

Louis sprayed most of his second sip of whisky out of his mouth on a choked splutter. He wiped his mouth with the back of his hand. 'Are you sure I'm the person you should be talking to about this?'

Her mouth was down-turned at the corners, her shoulders slumped. 'I'm still a virgin and I'm almost thirty. I need to do something to fix myself otherwise I'll never find a partner—especially today, when everyone's so adventurous and open about sex. I'm a pariah. An uptight prude who can't even get undressed unless the lights are out.'

To say he was shocked was an understatement. Almost thirty and still a virgin? He'd lost his in his teens. Didn't most people? She wasn't particularly religious, so deliberate abstinence could not be the issue. Had something happened to put her off doing the deed? His skin crawled at the thought of some pushy guy pressuring her or abusing her. Anger rose in his gut and climbed into his throat with acid-laced claws. Louis put down his glass of whisky and took a deep steadying breath.

'Firstly, Ivy, you don't have to fix anything. You should only do what you're comfortable doing when, and only when, you're comfortable doing it.'

'But I might never be comfortable if I don't do something sooner rather than later. I can't go on like this. It's beyond embarrassing going on a date with a new guy and then bolting out the door as soon as he touches me.'

Louis rapid blinked. Tried to ignore the little stab of unease in his gut about her hooking up with some guy she barely knew. 'Let me get this straight... You want *me* to *sleep* with you?'

Her cheeks darkened but her eyes contained a single-minded light that was more than a little unsettling. 'No one is never going to be interested in me unless I get over my inhibitions. There's no point me trying to date anyone unless I feel more confident. And I don't think I'd be comfortable with anyone but you. I know you. I've known you for years. Plus, you know what you're doing with sex, and I think you'd be the best person to teach me.'

A trap door creaked open in his mind, a narrow gap revealing a host of erotic possibilities he had locked down there, out of sight. Getting naked with her, doing all the things he'd been trying not to think about for the last couple of years. Gliding his hands down her beautiful body, exploring her breasts, discovering all the sweet contours of her feminine frame. Kissing her, touching her, their limbs entwined...

Louis held up his hand like a stop sign. 'Whoa there, Ivy. You're talking like a crazy person. I'm an architect, not a sex therapist. And, besides, we're friends. The friends-to-lovers thing never works.'

'But in this case it would work, because I'm not

after anything other than a one-night stand. That's what everyone calls you, right? Mr Amazing One-Night Stand. I'm not asking you to marry me. I just want you to have sex with me one time so I can say I'm not a virgin any—'

'I heard you the first time,' Louis cut in quickly. 'I'm not interested.' If he heard her ask him to have sex with her one more time, he'd be a goner. There was only so much self-control he could muster at a given time.

She looked like a puppy that had been refused a pat. Her teeth sank back into her bottom lip and she bent down to pick up her bag from the floor, where it had fallen earlier, and then straightened and levelled him with a wounded look. 'Is it because I'm not attractive enough? You find me a turn-off?'

Louis tried to keep his gaze away from her cleavage. Tried but failed. 'You're one of the most attractive women I've ever met but—'

'Prove it.' She put her bag on his desk and approached him. He had forgotten how tiny she was until she was toe-to-toe with him. She had to crane her neck to maintain eye contact. Her eyes were clear and her expression determined, and his self-control had a panic attack.

Louis cleared his suddenly tight throat. She was so close, if he moved half a step her breasts would brush his chest. He could see every pore of the creamy perfection of her skin, the only blemish a tiny white two-centimetre scar above her left eyebrow. Her blue eyes were an intricate mosaic of deep blue, purple and indigo with wide jet-black pupils as infinite as outer space. Her lower lip was twice the size of her top one, the shape of her mouth a perfect Cupid's bow. *And don't get me started about those adorable dimples.*

'Don't be ridiculous. I don't have to prove anything.' His tone was curt and cold but his blood was hot. Smoking hot. He placed his hands on her upper arms, ostensibly to keep her from him, but somehow his fingers sank into the softness of her cashmere sweater and the distance between their bodies closed. Had he moved or had she? Her hips brushed against his, her breasts poking into his chest, and a wave of hot, tight longing barrelled through him like a tornado.

'Kiss me, Louis.' Her voice was just shy of a whisper, her vanilla-scented breath dancing across his lips. 'Prove to me you don't find me a total turn-off.'

He'd kissed lots of women and had always been able to walk away. Always. It was his modus operandi. No strings. No follow-up dates. Just plain and simple one-night sex. But if he kissed Ivy he would be crossing a line he'd sworn he would never cross. He kept his relationships short—if you could call them relationships. Those 'relationships' were easy to walk away from without regret. But he already had a long-term relationship with Ivy. Not a sexual one, but a friendship that would be completely changed if he acted on her wishes. The last thing he wanted to do was rush into a one-night stand with Ivy until he understood exactly what she wanted from him.

His conscience leaned indolently against the back wall of his mind and smirked. *Oh, so you're actually going to consider sleeping with her?*

Louis summoned every bit of self-restraint he possessed and stepped back from her, dropping his hands from around her arms. He schooled his features into suave city playboy. 'If I kiss you, things could get hotter than you can handle. Are you sure you're ready for that, *ma petite*?'

A flicker of uncertainty passed over her face. 'Not completely, but if you won't do it then I'll have to resort to my Plan B.'

'Which is?'

Her small chin came up to a defiant height. 'I'll have to ask a stranger to do it.'

He held her gaze for a throbbing moment, his mind whirling with images of creepy strangers taking advantage of her guilelessness, and his guts churned with bile. No way was he going to let some filthy jerk touch her. There were some real weirdos out there these days, men who wanted to fulfil their darkest pornographic fantasies without considering their partner's wishes. Ivy wouldn't have the experience to handle something like that. It would totally destroy her.

'No, you will not do that.' He channelled his best schoolmaster voice, throwing in a deep frown for good measure.

Her expression became hopeful. 'So, you'll agree to help me?'

Louis speared a hand through his hair, then stood with his hands on his hips in a braced position. 'We'll come to that later. For now, I want to know why you got to the age of almost thirty with your virginity intact.'

Her gaze drifted away from his, her cheeks firing up again. 'I've always been a little bit uncomfortable even talking about sex, mostly because my mum has always been so out there about it—especially since she and Dad got divorced.' She glanced up at him. 'Did you know she's studying to be a sex therapist now? Sex is all she talks about.'

'Yeah, I heard about her new venture. But why not talk to her about…?'

A look of horror passed over her face. 'No way! I want to fix this on my own… Well, not quite on my own…with your help.'

He went back behind his desk and pulled out his office chair. 'Look, I'm on a tight deadline, but can we talk about this over dinner tonight? I'll pick you up at eight.'

Dinner? His conscience smirked again. *Dinner*

and then what? Dinner and nothing, that's what.
Nothing to see here, as the saying goes.

'Are you still in the flat in Islington?'

'Yep. My two friends Millie and Zoey have
moved in with me now. The rent on my own was
killing me.'

'Why didn't you say something? I could have
helped you.'

A glimmer of pride entered her gaze. 'You've
done enough for my family already—helping Mum
with the mortgage last year when she got behind
with the payments. She'll never be able to repay
you, you know. She's always been hopeless with
money.'

Louis' frown was back. Harder. Deeper. Seemed
no one kept a promise these days. He'd insisted
Deirdre Kennedy keep quiet about his offer to help
her out of yet another financial hole because he
genuinely hadn't wanted Ronan or Ivy to suffer any
more stress than they already had. He'd been particularly worried about Ronan. Finally coming out
to your divorced parents and then being rejected
by your father was enough to set off an existential
crisis in the most stable of people. It had taken the
best part of two years for him to feel comfortable
Ronan was out of danger.

Louis sat in his chair and absently straightened
some papers on his desk. 'She told you about that?'

Ivy nodded, her look grim. 'I forced it out of her. Ronan doesn't know, does he?'

He leaned back in his chair, picked up his fountain pen and rocked it back and forth between his thumb and index finger. 'It wasn't a big deal to me. It's just money. And I didn't want to worry you or Ronan. You had enough going on with your father's reaction to Ronan's situation.'

She gave a tight-lipped smile, but it was at odds with the shadow that passed through her gaze. 'All the same, it was nice of you to step in like that. Mum would have lost the house if it hadn't been for you.'

Louis let the pen drop back on the desk with a little clatter. 'Have you told Ronan about this harebrained scheme of yours?'

Ivy brought her gaze back to his. 'No. But he's hardly likely to find out now he's in Australia with Ricky. Anyway, he'd worry too much. He's been warning me for years about not getting fanciful ideas about you.'

'What fanciful ideas?' Louis knew he shouldn't ask.

'He said you weren't the marriage-and-babies type. But I told him not to worry about me because I would never be interested in a man who didn't want marriage and babies.'

If she mentioned 'marriage and babies' one more time he was going to blow a fuse. Not his most favourite words in the English language. His parents had married and had one baby and look how that had turned out. Thirty-five-plus years of misery for all concerned. 'I'm not sure falling in love works quite that way,' Louis pointed out. 'People fall in love with the wrong people all the time.' His parents being a case in point. Totally unsuited to each other but they soldiered on regardless. 'Soldiered' being a pertinent word, since every day was a battleground of injured egos, resentments, grievances and bitterness.

Ivy tilted her head and studied him for a moment. 'Have you ever been in love?'

'No.'

Her eyebrows rose. 'Not even once? Like when you were a teenager or…?'

'Nope.'

'But surely you must have felt a flicker of something for someone along the line?' She looked at him quizzically. 'You've had heaps of lovers. Have you just been using them all for sex?'

'Ahem, you're the one who wants to use me for sex, so don't go jumping up on your high horse just yet,' Louis said, holding her gaze.

She shifted her nose from side to side like a cute little bunny. 'It's not the same thing at all. I have an established relationship with you. You're like an older brother to me.' Her forehead creased in a tiny frown and she added, 'Well, maybe not so much a brother figure—because that would be kind of creepy and weird, having sex with you—but a good mate. Someone I can always rely on.'

A good mate would have stopped this conversation before it had got started. Drawn a thick black line through it. Frogmarched her out of his office and told her to go and get some therapy. Talking about this scheme of hers was like allowing a dangerous mind-altering vapour to infiltrate the air-conditioning. It was fuelling his forbidden fantasies, making it harder and harder to find a reason to say no. 'Have you told anyone about this plan of yours?'

'No. I wanted to ask you first.'

Louis leaned forward again and straightened the same papers next to his computer. 'I can't believe we're even having this conversation.' He glanced back at her with a stern frown. 'Are you sure you know what you're doing?'

Ivy picked up her bag from his desk and smiled so brightly she could have been advertising toothpaste. 'But that's the whole point—I don't know what I'm doing, but you're going to teach me.'

The scary thing was… Louis was seriously, dangerously, tempted to do exactly that.

CHAPTER TWO

IVY PUT THE last touches to her make-up in the bedroom at her flat before her dinner date with Louis. Dinner date. Such strange words to be using when it came to her relationship with Louis. Normally they had a quick catch-up over coffee or lunch. Dinner sounded a lot more…intimate. But she wasn't actually *dating* him. She was going to convince him to take her virginity, which would entail getting hot and sweaty with him.

A flutter of nerves erupted in her belly like a swarm of bumble bees. *Getting naked with him.* She smoothed a hand down her stomach. She hadn't got naked with anyone. She'd come close a couple of times but had freaked out. But any reservations she had would have to be put aside. She *had* to do this. How else would she gain the experience she needed? She couldn't face yet another dating disaster where a date wanted to take things to the next level and she bolted out the door like a Victorian prude.

The humiliating shame of her previous dates made her cringe on a daily basis. It had stopped her from venturing further into the dating world out of fear of further embarrassment. She'd had five dates and given up accepting any other invitations. Five dates! How pathetic was that? She didn't know why she had become so sensually locked down but, ever since she'd hit puberty, the thought of sharing her body with someone had paralysed her with fear.

What if they didn't like her body? What if she wasn't the right shape or size? What if she didn't do or say the right thing and they thought her a freak? What if she fell in love and got rejected like her mother had got rejected by her father?

Every time she went on a date those fears would flap through her brain like a swarm of frenzied bats. *What if? What if? What if?* It made it impossible to think of anything else but escaping as soon as she could. Not exactly the best way to find the life partner you'd been dreaming of finding since you'd been a little girl.

But her plan to get Louis to help her was a masterstroke of genius. He was exactly the right person to help her overcome this hurdle of intimacy avoidance. Then she would be free to search for Mr Right.

One of her flatmates, Millie, peered round Ivy's bedroom door. 'Woo-hoo. You look gorgeous. Are you going on a date?' She waggled her eyebrows meaningfully.

'Don't get too excited. It's not really a date.' Ivy put her lip-gloss back in her cosmetics bag. 'I'm going out for dinner with Louis Charpentier.'

Millie came further into the bedroom, eyebrows raised. 'Your brother's friend? The four-times-and-counting hot bachelor of the year? For dinner? How is that not a date?'

Ivy adjusted her little black dress over her hips. 'We're just…catching up.'

Millie's gaze ran over Ivy's outfit and make-up. 'Mmm, methinks you've gone to a lot of trouble for a simple catch-up with a friend. Are you sure nothing's going on?'

Ivy flicked an imaginary piece of lint off her shoulder. 'Of course, I'm sure. It's not a big deal. Louis likes to check up on me now and again now that Ronan's living in Sydney.'

Millie gave a light laugh. 'Gosh, I would love someone as hot as Louis Charpentier to check up on me every now and again. What do you two talk about when you get together?'

'Just…stuff. Movies, books, work—that sort of thing.' A trickle of fear slithered its way down Ivy's spine. What had she got herself in to? She was actually *going to have sex*. With her brother's best friend. *Eek*. Ivy felt bad about not being totally truthful with her friend. Why should it matter if she told Millie about her plan? But surely the less people who knew, the better? It was a one-off thing with Louis. No point allowing her friends to think it was anything else.

Millie leaned down and peered into Ivy's face. 'Why are you blushing?'

'I'm not blushing.' Ivy might as well not have bothered with using blusher, the way her cheeks were feeling.

Millie straightened and folded her arms. 'Come on. Fess up. What is going on with you and Louis?'

Ivy should know it was virtually impossible to keep a secret from Millie. Her friend was like a sniffer dog for secrets. The trouble was, she wasn't so good at keeping them. Ivy met her friend's gaze and released a sigh. 'He's helping me with something.'

Millie frowned. 'What something? Has your mum been leaning on you for money again?'

'No. It's about me. About my…problem.'

Millie's eyes widened to the size of light bulbs. Football-stadium light bulbs. 'The V problem? Seriously—you're asking him to do what, exactly?'

'I'm going to have a one-night stand with him. Then my problem will be solved.'

'And he's agreed to that?'

'Not in so many words, hence dinner tonight. But I'm not going to let him talk me out of it. He's the only person who can help me. The only person I *want* to help me. I'd be too embarrassed or shy with anyone else.'

Millie's expression was etched in concern. 'But what if you develop feelings for him? I mean, different from what you have for him now?'

Ivy laughed, picked up her hairbrush and began stroking it through her hair. 'You mean like fall in love with him? Not a chance. He's not the settling down type. It would be stupid to fall in love with him, knowing he doesn't want the same things in life that I do. Louis only has one-nighters. I want someone who's there for the long haul. Someone who'll stick around no matter what—unlike my father. Not that Louis is anything like my father, but you know what I mean. Once a playboy, always a playboy.'

Millie's expression was so sceptical she could have been keynote speaker at a sceptics' conference. 'What your father's done really sucks, but have you actually looked at Louis lately? I mean, *really* looked at him? The man is traffic-stopping gorgeous.'

'I know, but I don't think of him that way,' Ivy said, spraying perfume on her pulse points. She wasn't sure why she didn't see Louis the way other women did…although there had been a strange little flicker of something when their hands had touched that afternoon. A tingle travelled up her arm like a current of electricity. And when he'd used a French term of endearment, well, what girl wouldn't have got a shiver down her spine? But her preference had always been for blond men and Louis, with his Anglo-French ancestry, had pitch-black hair. Not her type at all.

'You might think of him that way once you get naked with him.'

Get naked with him. The words made her skin lift in a delicate shiver. Ivy put the perfume bottle down with a definitive clunk. 'Not going to happen. This is just about sex, nothing else.'

'So how long are you going to be sleeping with him?'

'Just for one night.'

Ivy picked up her evening bag and smoothed her hand over her fluttering stomach. *If I can convince him and then have the guts to go through with it.*

'Wish me luck?'

Millie gave her a long, searching look. 'You're going to need more than luck. You're the last person on earth—apart from me, of course—who's a one-night stand sort of person. People are always telling me to move on from losing Julian but it's too hard these days to find someone who doesn't expect you to put out before you even get to know them.'

Millie had tragically lost her fiancé, Julian, to brain cancer only weeks before their wedding three years ago. His battle to fight it had been long and gruelling and it was heartbreakingly sad Millie hadn't got to marry her childhood sweetheart before he died. Apart from a disastrous blind date set up by another friend a couple of months ago, Millie had point-blank refused to think of finding room in her heart for anyone else.

Ivy took Millie's hand and gave it a squeeze. 'What you had with Jules was really special, and I don't blame you for finding it hard to think of moving on. But don't you see? I want that sort of love one day too, but I won't find it spending yet another weekend at home alone watching box sets.'

Millie touched Ivy on the arm, her expression serious. 'Are you sure you're doing the right thing? This might change your relationship with Louis for ever. Are you prepared to risk that?'

Ivy straightened her shoulders. 'I have to do this, Millie. I want to be able to date a guy without my inexperience hanging over me and this is the best way to do it.' She leaned forward and kissed her friend on the cheek. 'But thanks for being concerned about me.'

The doorbell sounded at that moment and Ivy's stomach pitched. 'That'll be Louis.' She waved a hand on her way out of the bedroom. 'Don't wait up!'

Louis had lost count of the number of times he'd taken a woman out to dinner, so there was no reason why this time he should be feeling as if this date was something special.

Date? Is that what this is?

No. It. Was. Not. He hadn't committed to anything. One part of him was determined to talk Ivy out of her plan to have him initiate her into the joy of sex, the other part of him was mentally stockpiling condoms and scented candles. What had got into him? Where were his set-in-stone boundaries?

Louis adjusted his tie and then pressed the doorbell on Ivy's flat. The sound of heels click-clacking on floorboards sent his pulse up. Was it his imagination or could he already smell her perfume? The door opened and Ivy stood there in a little black dress that clung to every delicious curve on her body, the vertiginous heels she was wearing showcasing her slim legs and ankles. Her hair was loose around her shoulders, and his fingers itched so much to reach out and touch it, he had to shove his hands into his trouser pockets.

'Hiya.' Her lips curved around a smile and desire coiled hot and tight in his groin. Her smoky eye make-up made her periwinkle-blue eyes look all the more stunning, and her shimmering lipgloss highlighted the perfect shape of her mouth. Her utterly kissable, sexy-as-hell mouth. Heaven help him.

'Good evening.' Louis stretched his mouth into one of his carefully rationed smiles. 'You look amazing.'

Amazing, sexy, gorgeous, stunning, beautiful...

The words piled into his brain as if he had swallowed a thesaurus. She didn't look like his friend's sister any more, which was a problem, because he needed to get those boundaries firmly back in place. And fast.

'Thank you.'

There was a funny little silence.

'Right. Well, then.' Louis took his hands out of his pockets and gestured towards the street where his car was parked. 'Shall we go?'

Ivy stepped down the three steps to the footpath but almost stumbled on the last one and Louis shot out one of his hands to stabilise her. 'Whoa, there. Take it easy in those shoes. How on earth do you walk in them?' His fingers moved from grasping her wrist to curl around hers and another punch of lust hit him in the groin.

'I like wearing heels. It makes me taller. Otherwise I'd end up with neckache trying to look up at people all the time, particularly people as tall as you.'

He kept hold of her hand on the way to his car. Her fingers were soft as silk and her hand so small it was completely swallowed up by his. 'I'll have to get you a stepladder or something when you're with me. I don't want you to break your ankle on my behalf.'

She gave a tinkling-bell laugh and playfully

shoulder bumped him. 'Don't be silly. So, where are we having dinner? I'm starving.'

'A French restaurant.'

She grinned up at him. 'So you can dazzle me with your fluent French?'

'Something like that.' Louis was the one being dazzled. Big time. He knew he was crazy even to take her out to dinner, let alone contemplate anything else. She was exactly the type of girl he avoided—the type who wanted the husband, the house and the sleepy hound in front of the cosy fireplace. He'd missed out on the settling-down gene, or had had it pummelled out of him through witnessing the marital misery of his parents. These days the sense of claustrophobia at being in a relationship longer than twenty-four hours was suffocating. He enjoyed sex for the physical relief it gave but, since his stalker, the thought of a longer relationship made him break out into hives.

In his opinion, long-term commitment was a dirty word.

Louis helped her into the passenger seat and tried not to notice how her black dress revealed a tiny shadow of cleavage and a whole lot of her shapely thighs. Tried to ignore the way his pulse shot up and his blood thickened.

He strode to the driver's side and gave himself a stern talking to.

It's just dinner. Nothing else. You're going to talk her out of her crazy plan, remember?

'Louis?'

He flicked her a quick glance as the engine turned over. 'Yes?'

Her fingers were fiddling with the clasp on her evening bag, her cheeks a faint shade of pink. 'Do you carry condoms with you all the time?'

He stared blankly at her for a moment. 'Ah, well, yes, but we're not going to need them tonight.'

'But why not?'

His hands gripped the steering wheel so hard his knuckles threatened to burst out of his skin. And that wasn't the only part of his anatomy fit to burst. The stirring in his groin sent hot tingles down his legs at the thought of making love to her. He met her gaze. 'We're not going to have sex, Ivy. Not tonight, not tomorrow, not—'

'Why not? I bet you have sex with other women on the first date.'

'This isn't a date,' he said through tight lips. 'It's a meeting to discuss your…situation.'

'My situation is that I want you to take my virginity. Why are you being so…so difficult about this?'

He sent her a sideways glance. 'You're not the one-night-stand type. You've got no experience of how to do this sort of hook-up.'

'Which is why I want you to give it to me.'

Louis clenched his jaw so hard, he thought he was going to crack his mandible. 'Look, I think we should talk about it some more before we go rushing into something with so many pitfalls. If we sleep together, it will change everything. We will never look at each other the same way again.'

'Does it matter? I mean, you have sex with heaps of women and it doesn't seem to be a problem.' She let out a whooshing sigh. 'Maybe it's *me* that's the problem. I'm so undesirable you can't bear the thought of touching me.'

If only it were that simple. He'd been fighting the temptation to touch her since she'd come into his office that afternoon. He was fighting it now. She was the most desirable woman he'd met in a long time. 'Feeling desire for someone doesn't mean I'll act on it. Not unless I'm convinced it's the right thing to do.'

'How else can I convince you? Do you know how embarrassing it is for me to be the only person in my circle of friends who's still a virgin? I can't imagine asking anyone else to help me. I would be too embarrassed—or at least more embarrassed, because it certainly wasn't easy asking you this afternoon. Hence the brandy. Imagine if I had to ask a stranger!'

His gut roiled at the thought of her going out with a stranger. Doing *anything* with a stranger. Louis forced himself to relax his grip on the steering wheel. 'I don't think we should rush into this without some proper checks and balances done first.'

'Fine. But let's not take too long about it—because I turn thirty in a month and no way am I going to celebrate my birthday as a flipping virgin.' She blew out a breath and continued, 'I know this has come as a shock to you, but I've been struggling with this for years. I hate it that I can be so confident at work but this area of my life is so stuffed up. I need to get past this in order to move on with my life. It's like there's a big fat pause button on my future. Solving this will press the go switch, I'm sure of it.'

Yes, but it was the 'go' switch he was most worried about. Worried about removing the boundaries he had set up. Relaxing his self-control. Doing things with her he had only done in his most wicked dreams.

She suddenly flashed him a teasing smile. 'Are you worried you might fall for me? Is that where your reluctance is coming from?'

He gave her the side-eye. 'I know how to keep my feelings in check.' He'd been doing it most of his life. Controlling his reaction to his father's acid tongue and overly critical eye. Ignoring his father's repeated digs about his choice of career and how he had let everybody down by not joining the family accounting business as expected. Ignoring his mother's incessant nit-picking over every aspect of his life, knowing deep down it was her way of compensating for her lack of power in her marriage, and her bitter disappointment at only having one child after several miscarriages.

He had witnessed way too many of his parents' fights in which bitter words had been exchanged, but one in particular had stuck in his mind as a ten-year-old child, so too the harrowing aftermath. His mother's admission into a mental health clinic for months on end after a suicide attempt. Louis had shut down his feelings at seeing his mother inside the walls of a locked mental-health unit. Her blank, flat look—as if someone had pulled out the power cord to her personality. He had suppressed his own despair in order to cope with his father's. When his mother had finally come home, his father had grov-elled, begged, over-adapted and promised things he could never deliver.

That was forever love? Louis wanted nothing to do with it.

'I sometimes wish I could keep my feelings in check…' Ivy's tone contained a self-deprecating note. 'Ronan's always telling me I wear my heart on my sleeve. Both sleeves, actually.'

Louis glanced at her. 'Have you heard from your father lately?'

She sighed and looked down at her hands in her lap. 'No. I think he's blocked me on his phone. It's much worse for Ronan. The things Dad said to him were unforgiveable. I was really worried about him there for a bit.'

'Yeah, so was I.' Louis pulled into a parking spot near the restaurant and turned off the engine. 'But he seems happy now with Ricky.'

She swivelled in her seat to look at him. 'Louis?'

'Yes?'

Her eyes went to his mouth and a small frown settled on her forehead. The tip of her tongue came out and licked her lips, and scorching heat flooded his groin. The air tightened and the space between them shrank, his self-control wavering like a slab of concrete on a building site held by a gossamer thread. It would be so easy to reach for her hand, to stroke the creamy curve of her cheek, to lean forward and press his lips against the plump ripeness of hers. He could feel the magnetic pull of attraction drawing him closer, every cell in his body poised, primed for contact. In his mind he was already doing it—kissing her until they were both breathless, his tongue tangling with hers, his blood pounding like a tribal drum.

Go on, do it. You know you want to.

Her gaze met his and she gave one of her dazzling, dimpled smiles. 'Hey, for a moment there I thought you were going to kiss me.'

Louis traced the curve of her mouth with a lazy finger, fizzing sensations shooting through him. 'I was definitely thinking about it.' His voice was so rough it sounded as if he'd been snacking on gravel.

'Then why don't you do it?' Her voice was not much more than a breathy whisper that sent a wave of hot tingles across his scalp and down his spine.

He leaned across the gear shift and lowered his head until his mouth was barely an inch from hers. Her breath was milk and honey with a dash of cinnamon-sweetness, innocent, addictive. 'Once I kiss you, I can't *un*-kiss you.'

Her fan-like eyelashes came down over her eyes and her right hand came up and slid along the side of his face, the soft skin of her palm and fingers catching on his light stubble like fine silk on sandpaper. 'You worry too much.' She closed the distance between their mouths and touched his lips with the rose-petal softness of hers. It was the barest of touchdowns, but an explosion of sensation erupted in his lips. She eased back to look at him, her eyes dark and luminous. 'See? No harm done. It was just a kiss.'

Just a kiss? Her lips were a drug he hadn't known he had a weakness for until now. Before he could stop himself, Louis put a hand behind her head, splaying his fingers through the wild curls of her hair. Her mouth opened on a soft little gasp, as if his touch electrified her the same as hers did him.

He lowered his mouth to hers in achingly slow

motion, drawn by a force as old as time. An irre-sistible force that sent his blood roaring through his veins and his willpower flying out the window. His lips finally met hers and incendiary heat charged from her mouth to his. He gave a low, deep groan and increased the pressure of his lips on hers, fu-elled by an uncontrollable need for closer, firmer contact. Her mouth opened beneath the insistent pressure of his, her tongue brushing shyly against his. He cradled one side of her face, the other hand still buried in the red-gold tresses of her fragrant hair, his kiss deepening, his desire rising, his self-control wavering.

Ivy whimpered against his mouth, her hands coming up around his neck, her fingers playing with his short-cropped hair.

Every hair on his head tingled at the roots, every nerve in his body was on high alert, every reason for not sleeping with her retreating to the back of his mind. He breathed in the scent of her—spring flow-ers with an undertone of heady, intoxicating musk. Somehow, he sucked in some much-needed air be-fore taking the kiss a step further, his tongue duel-ling with hers in a sexy tango that made his blood thunder through his body. Every time his tongue touched hers, a zapping lightning bolt of lust fired through him. Her lips were velvet-soft and he could taste her strawberry lip-gloss and his own salty, earthy and raw desire—a lethal blend of temptation.

He knew he would never be able to eat a strawberry again without thinking of their first kiss.

Without thinking of *her*.

The thought was sobering enough to give him pause. He pulled back from her, lowering his hands from her cheek and the back of her head, his breathing still out of order, his body still roaring with lust. She looked as dazed as he felt—her eyes shining, her lips cherry-red and swollen, her cheeks tinged with pink.

'Well, that was a surprise.' Her tone was light, but a small frown appeared between her neat eyebrows and her gaze drifted back to his mouth. She moistened her lips with a quick dart of her tongue, her gaze coming back to his. 'I didn't think it would be as…as nice as that.'

'What? You haven't enjoyed being kissed before?'

'Not really, but with you it was…something else.' She touched her fingers to her lips as if she couldn't quite believe what had happened. Her fingers fell away and she added, 'Is it my imagination or was that kiss kind of off the charts?'

Louis fought not to smile. 'It was pretty damn good. You certainly don't need any tutoring in that department.'

She cocked her head like an inquisitive little bird. 'Hey, is that a smile you're trying to hide?' Her own mouth was curved in a smile that made something warm spread through his chest. But he could and would keep his emotions out of this. He did it all the time. A kiss was just a kiss. He wasn't going to commit to anything else that could have more troubling consequences. He unclipped his seatbelt and took the wireless car-key out of its slot on the dashboard. 'Come on. Let's eat. I'm starving.'

But it wasn't a physical hunger gnawing at him. It was good old-fashioned, rip-roaring lust.

Ivy was still reliving every moment of their kiss when they were shown to their table in the fancy French restaurant in Soho. Their table was in a secluded part of the restaurant and she wondered if Louis had requested it especially to avoid public scrutiny. She knew he wasn't fond of the attention his high-profile career as an award-winning architect occasionally attracted from the press. She herself had been guilty of poring over articles about him online, but mostly in a he's-my-brother's-best-friend-and-I'm-proud-of-his-achievements sort of way. Nothing else. She had zero interest in him romantically...although that kiss had certainly been a bit of an eye-opener. Her lips were still tingling, along with other parts of her body that had rarely, if ever, tingled before.

Louis looked up from his perusal of the menu. 'Is there anything that you particularly fancy?'

You. Ivy was a little shocked at how much she

fancied him. Up until recently, he had simply been her brother's best friend—the person she could always rely on to help her, which was why she had approached him with 'the V plan'. But that kiss had changed something inside her. Maybe Louis was right—they wouldn't be able to go back to the way they'd been. Changing the dynamic of a relationship—any relationship—was something that could be risky.

She wasn't the greatest fan of change. She'd been in the same job since university, she'd had the same friends since school. She hadn't coped well with her parents' divorce when she'd been a teenager. She hated moving house. She couldn't pack a bag for a weekend away without worrying she might leave something behind that she needed.

But hadn't things already changed between them? How could she see Louis as anyone other than the first man who had set her mouth on fire? Lust was a new experience for her. Her previous dates hadn't stirred anywhere near the same sensations in her body—she hadn't felt a thing from any of them. She had learned from her parents' divorce that the last thing she wanted to do was develop feelings for someone who couldn't love her back. But all Louis had done was kiss her and she was hot for him. She could still taste him in her mouth, could still feel the brush of his hand against her face, his fingers buried in her hair.

She shivered and buried her head in the menu, wondering if her cheeks were as warm as they felt. 'Let me see, now... Snails? Frogs' legs? Steak tartare?'

'Tell me you're joking.' His tone was so dry it could have mopped up an oil spill.

Ivy gave him a cheeky smile. 'I'm joking. But, hey, what sort of Frenchman are you to turn your nose up at *escargots*?'

'I'm only half-French. My mother is English.' He picked up the wine list and opened it. 'The only time I ate snails was when my father insisted on it when I was six years old.'

'And?'

He didn't stop looking at the menu, but she had a feeling he wasn't registering a single word written there. His features tightened as if he was trying to keep an unpleasant memory contained. 'I was violently ill.'

'Are you allergic to them or something?'

Louis put the menu down and met her gaze with a now bland expression. 'No. But, since they're my father's favourite dish, I was left in no doubt of how much I'd disappointed him.' He tapped the wine menu with his fingers. 'Champagne or white wine... or how about some brandy?' His grey-blue eyes glinted and something between her legs fluttered like the wings of a moth.

Ivy shifted in her seat, winding her mind back to

his earlier comment rather than examine too closely what her body was currently doing. 'I'll have white wine. What are your parents like? You've never told me anything about them before. Are you close to them?'

He gave a soft grunt that said everything that needed to be said. So too did the bitter twist of his mouth and the ripple of tension along his jaw. 'I have very little in common with either of them other than DNA.'

The waiter came for the drinks order at that moment and it gave Ivy a chance to surreptitiously study Louis. It occurred to her that she had known him for years—close to a decade—and yet there was still so much about him she didn't know. He was a reserved type of man, similar to her brother Ronan, which had strengthened the bond between them during her brother's difficult time in finally embracing his sexuality. But she hadn't known anything about Louis' relationship with his family other than he was an only child and that his father ran a large international accounting firm with branches throughout Europe. The unknown aspect of Louis' character was a timely reminder not to allow her feelings to get involved. But, perversely, it made her all the more fascinated by him. Who was he behind the Mr Amazing One-Night Stand persona?

The waiter left and Ivy picked up the conversation again. 'Do your parents live here or in France?'

'They split their time between the two,' Louis said. 'My father inherited my grandparents' chateau in the Loire valley when they died a few years ago. It's been in our family for five generations.'

'So, being their only child, you'll inherit it one day?'

He gave her an inscrutable look. 'Perhaps.'

Ivy wrinkled her forehead in a frown. 'Perhaps? What does that mean?'

He let out a slow breath and moved his water glass a quarter turn. 'It means my father is likely to change his mind after some perceived slight from me, so I don't have any expectations in that regard. I've made my own money. I don't need his.'

Ivy picked up her own glass of water. 'Gosh, and here I was thinking my father was a pain in the butt.' She took a sip of water before putting the glass back down. 'Not that he was always like that...'

Louis met her gaze. 'Do you miss him? Ronan told me you used to be really close to him before your parents divorced.'

She found it hard to hold his gaze and looked at the small flower arrangement on the table instead. Her parents divorcing when she was thirteen had been tough, but her father's rejection of her because of her loyalty to her brother had been the hardest thing she had ever faced. Her father's love was something she'd thought she'd always be able to rely on, but she'd been wrong. His ultimatum that she cease all contact with Ronan otherwise never see him again had totally blindsided her. To be made to choose between her adored older brother and equally adored father was beyond cruel.

'I thought he loved me. I really did. I thought he loved both of us, and Mum too back in the day. He used to say Mum's quirkiness and out-there personality was what attracted him in the first place, but where was his love for her when he had that affair when I was thirteen? Their divorce was bad enough but at least I still got to spend time with my dad on weekend access visits. I never doubted his love for me and Ronan. But, since Ronan told us he was gay two years ago, Dad turned off his love for us like turning off a light switch. I still can't quite get my head around it. I mean, we're his flesh and blood, and yet he refuses to have anything to do with us. I feel like I've loved someone all my life that I didn't really know at all.'

Louis reached across the table and covered her hand with the broad expanse of his. The skin on the back of her hand tingled, the hairs on the back of her neck standing up, the soft flutter between her legs returning. His eyes were an intense smoky blue—clouds and sky, shadows and sunlight, unknowable depths and shifting shallows.

'I'm sorry you've been so hurt by him. But it's

his problem, not yours. You have to remember you and Ronan did nothing wrong.'

Ivy gave him a wry smile. 'You should have been a therapist.'

His gaze dipped to her mouth for a brief moment, his own mouth twisting in a rueful half-smile. He removed his hand from hers and sat back in his chair. 'Yes, well, I've been handling difficult people all my life.'

Ivy wanted to ask more about his family, but just then the waiter came back with their wine and, once it was poured, he took their meal order before discreetly melting away again.

Ivy picked up her glass and raised it in a toast. 'What shall we drink to? One night without strings?' On the surface she sounded cool and calm about sleeping with him but on the inside her nerves were going haywire. What if she freaked out just as she had the other times? But then she recalled their kiss and thought maybe she wouldn't freak out. Maybe making love with him would be like kissing him—wonderful, amazing. But how would she know without convincing him to do it?

Louis' mouth flattened. 'Here's the thing—it's never without strings. It's rare for two people to want the same thing out of a fling, no matter how short it is.'

'But as long as we're clear on the rules from the outset why should it be a problem? I mean, we're not strangers—we're friends who will continue to have a relationship once our night together is over.'

One of his ink-black eyebrows rose in a sceptical arc. 'Will we?'

'Of course,' Ivy said. 'Why wouldn't we? You're Ronan's best friend. I will never forget how much you've supported him over the years. You were the first person he came out to, years before he told anyone else. I truly think he wouldn't have made it without your support and acceptance.'

'Which is why I'm concerned about this plan of yours.' His expression was etched in lines of gravitas. 'What if it proves too awkward to go back to being friends?'

Ivy let out a gusty sigh. Was this going to be the story of her life? Constant rejection? 'I think you're looking for excuses not to sleep with me. All right. You win. Forget about my plan. I'll find someone else.'

There was a tight silence.

Louis reached for her hand again, his fingers warm and strong over hers. 'No. Don't do that.' His eyes held hers in an unwavering lock. 'I'm still getting my head around what you want from me.'

'Why? Because I have sexual needs just like anyone else?' Ivy asked, pulling her hand out of his. 'I'm not a child, Louis. I'm a fully-grown woman and I want to feel like one in bed with a man. But how can I if I freak out at the thought of undressing in front of a guy?'

'Have you gone on any dates in the past?'

'Four.' Ivy mentally cringed at her paltry number of dates. No doubt Louis' dates numbered six figures by now.

'Only four?'

'Yep, and they were all disasters.'

His dark brows drew together, a shadow of concern backlighting his gaze. 'Why?'

Ivy released a heavy sigh. 'The first one of my dates asked me out for a drink. That was fine until he said he forgot his wallet and he suggested we swing by his house and…'

'You didn't go with him, did you?' His frown was deeper, almost savage in its intensity.

Ivy wasn't sure how to answer. How could she tell him she was afraid of trusting someone enough to let them get that close to her? As physically close as two people could be? Not just physically close but emotionally close. That was even more terrifying. 'Well, I was so new to dating, I didn't really know what else to do. He asked me out, so I went with him out of politeness. But once we got to his flat he tried to kiss me and touch me and I found it all a bit too much too soon. The second date was a bit better but ended much the same. We met for a drink and then went to a nightclub and then went back to his place.'

'Did he pressure you to go home with him?'

'Not really. I wanted to go. I actually liked him more than the other guy. I thought there was some potential there for a proper relationship. We kissed a bit, but I can't say I enjoyed it. And as soon as he started to undress me I freaked out. It was so embarrassing. He must have thought I was a crazy person. I bolted out the door and caught a cab home. The other dates were much the same. I'd be sort of fine until it came to the kissing and touching part and then I would freeze or run. I haven't dated anyone since. I'm rubbish at it, which is why I have to do something about it before it's too late.'

'It sounds to me like you've had a bunch of crap dates. You shouldn't let it put you off dating again.'

Ivy's shoulders slumped on a sigh. 'I'm not confident enough to date someone I don't know. But how can I get to know someone if I don't date them? It's an impossible situation.'

There was a silence.

He picked up his wine glass but didn't raise it to his mouth. 'Maybe I can help you with that.'

Ivy's eyes flicked back to his. 'How?'

His eyes drifted to her mouth once more. 'We could go on some dates together, to help you build your confidence around men.'

'You mean sleep with me? You'll actually do…?'

He held up his hand like a stop sign. 'Wait. Hear me out.' He lowered his hand to the table. 'I think what's happened with your last dates is, you felt pressured the whole time about having sex straight up. What might help is spending time with me— for instance, where sex is a possibility rather than a given.'

Ivy frowned. 'Sex as a possibility? Seriously, is that what you think every time you go on a date, Mr Amazing One-Night Stand?'

He gave her a mock glower. 'Not usually, but neither do I pressure a woman to have sex if I don't think she wants the same thing. You and I can spend a bit of time together to help you feel more in control.'

Maybe he had a point. The possibility of sex might somehow be less threatening than the certainty of it... And yet strangely, because it would be Louis and not some other guy she was randomly dating, she wanted certainty. 'Okay. So, where will we go?'

'Look, if we're going to do this, then I think we need to keep a low profile. I don't want the press sniffing around and it getting back to Ronan.'

Ivy could understand his guardedness on one level but another part of her wondered if his reluctance to be seen in public with her had more to do with her looks. She wasn't his usual type. He went for tall and tanned leggy blondes, and she was short and curvy, her hair was red and her skin as white as milk. Not exactly billboard model material.

'Fine. We can do that. When do we start?'

He took a deep sip of his wine before he answered. 'Are you free this Friday night?'

Ivy rolled her eyes. 'I'm free *every* Friday night. That's the whole problem.'

A smile played at the edges of his mouth. 'I don't know what's wrong with the young men in London to overlook you for all this time.'

She gave him a rueful glance. 'It's not the young men that's the problem. It's me. I've refused heaps of offers of dates. But hopefully you'll be able to fix me.'

His smile faded and a frown appeared on his forehead. 'You don't need fixing, Ivy. There's nothing wrong with you.'

'What if I'm frigid? What if I can't get over my inhibitions?'

'We'll work on building your confidence first and I bet the rest will sort itself out.'

Ivy grasped his hand across the table. 'Thank you.'

He picked up her hand and brought it up to his lips, holding her gaze with the grey-blue intensity of his. He pressed a soft-as-air kiss to her bent knuckles, sending a wave of heat through her entire body. Electric fizzes and tingles that made her acutely aware of the throbbing pulse deep and low in her pelvis. She couldn't break his gaze even if she'd wanted to. She was transfixed by the naked need she could see reflected there, the same need she could feel vibrating in her body.

But he still hadn't fully committed to sleeping with her and the clock was ticking as she approached her thirtieth birthday. *Tick. Tick. Tick.* What if he refused to do as she asked? What if his 'possibility of sex' became an impossibility for him? The thought of hooking up with a stranger was even more distressing to her now, especially since she had been kissed by Louis. His kiss had surprised and delighted her in a way no other kiss had. Her previous dates had kissed her, but those kisses hadn't been a patch on Louis'. He'd suggested spending time together first, and that sounded all fine and dandy, but what she wanted—needed—was to offload her inhibitions. And the only way to do that was to get the deed done. With him.

The moment was broken by the waiter turning up with their entrée but, all through the rest of the meal, Ivy was conscious of Louis' every movement. It was as if her body's radar had a new setting, aware of him in a way it hadn't been before. His hands as he operated his cutlery. The movement of his lips as he took a sip of wine. The way his crisp ice-blue business shirt framed his broad shoulders and muscular chest. The tan of his skin that hinted at the amount of time he spent outdoors. The long, straight blade of his nose, the aristocratic contour of his cheekbones, the dark slash of his eyebrows above his sharply intelligent eyes.

As far as the male package went, he had everything—looks, wealth, stability, sex appeal. Why hadn't she noticed that brooding sex appeal before? Or maybe she had but had dismissed it, thinking he would never be interested in her.

But he *was* interested in her. His kiss had proved that without a doubt. The chemistry between them was unmistakable, obvious even to someone with as little experience as her.

Ivy picked up her napkin and dabbed at each corner of her mouth. 'Just out of interest—have you ever made love to a virgin before?'

Louis blinked as if her question had startled him out of a private reverie. 'No.' He put down his knife and fork in the 'finished' position on his dinner plate.

Ivy picked up her wine glass, a strange tickly sensation trickling down the back of her legs. 'Does the thought of doing so make you nervous?'

His eyes came back to hers and another jolting sensation pulsed through her body. 'No. I can see now how much your virginity is troubling you.'

She studied him for a moment. 'So, you're really serious about helping me?'

'One thing you should know about me, *ma ché-*

rie. Once I commit to a goal, I always see it through. Always.'

Ivy suppressed a delicious shudder. *Lucky me.*

CHAPTER THREE

'So how did your dinner with Louis Charpentier go?' Zoey, her other flatmate, asked the next morning. 'I hope you don't mind, but Millie told me about "the plan". Did he agree to it?'

So much for keeping her plan a secret. One thing was certain, Millie would never cut it as an undercover agent. 'Yes and no. I think he's stalling but I'm going to change his mind. I have to. I've only got a month to get this done.' Ivy reached for a coffee pod and popped it in the machine. 'We're going out on Friday night.' Saying those words out loud made her body tingle all over in anticipation. Louis hadn't touched her again after he'd dropped her home the night before, and it surprised her how much she'd wanted him to.

'Ooh! Where's he taking you?' Zoey leaned on the counter near the coffee machine, her own steaming cup cradled in her hands.

'I don't know. He didn't say.' Ivy spoke over

the noise of the coffee machine. 'Do you think I'm crazy to ask him to help me?'

'Not really,' Zoey said. 'You're friends, so you already trust him. That's huge when it comes to physical intimacy.'

'He's not actually agreed to sleep with me, or at least not on the first date. He just wants to spend time with me first with sex being a possibility rather than a given. He thinks it will help me to gain more confidence around men.'

'Listen, honey, if a man wants to spend time with you he wants to sleep with you.' Zoey's tone was dry.

Ivy was still in two minds about what Louis wanted. On the one hand, she was certain he wanted to make love to her, but on the other hand, she suspected he was feeling too conflicted to act on his desire. Her job was to change his mind one way or the other. 'Millie thinks I might fall in love with him and get my heart broken.'

Zoey studied her for a moment. 'Do you think that's a possibility?'

'I don't think so. I'm not attracted to love-them-and-leave-them playboys.' She chewed at her lower lip and stirred her coffee. 'I've known Louis for close to a decade and never once felt anything for him other than friendship.'

Apart from the moment she'd walked into his office. And at dinner. Not to mention *the kiss*. And every time he dropped a French endearment her way.

'Why should that change if we did have a one-night stand?' Why should that change after one kiss? But, niggling doubts aside, she couldn't back out now. She wanted to see this through no matter what. It was imperative she get herself sorted out and no one could help her better than Louis.

Zoey plonked her cup down and pushed herself away from the bench. 'It's a risk, I guess. Good sex can have a potent effect on your emotions. Not that I've had any lately, but nor do I want any. I'm completely over men.'

Ivy knew her friend was still getting over the betrayal of her long-term boyfriend who had cheated on her while she'd been away with her father on business. Zoey was still in a man-hating phase even though it had been over a year since she'd found out about the affair. 'How did your dinner with your dad go?'

Zoey sighed and picked up a piece of toast. 'He drank too much and I had to bundle him into a taxi. Same old.' She bit into the toast as if she wanted to hurt it, her stunning violet eyes shadowed with decades-old pain.

'Oh, dear.'

Ivy knew all about embarrassing parents. Her mother had struggled, self-medicating with alcohol and casual affairs with multiple partners, after Ivy's dad had left when she was a teenager. Her mother had only ever had one lover until then—Ivy's father—so it had been weird seeing her mother with a host of men she'd met in a pub or wine bar. Ivy had never known who she would meet on her way to the bathroom or what sounds she would hear coming from her mother's bedroom. None of the men had stayed around longer than a night or two before someone else would appear.

'I'm worried it's going to affect the business,' Zoey went on. 'I've had to cover for him so many times lately.' She speared a hand through her thick, glossy black hair, her expression troubled. 'It's like he's self-sabotaging what he's worked so hard for all his life. I can't stand by and watch him destroy the company. It's my company too—or it would be if he'd change his mind and make me a partner.'

'Oh, Zoey, I wish I could say something that would help. It must be so awful for you.'

Zoey stretched her mouth into an on-off smile. 'Don't mind me, I'm just venting. The thing that gets me is the blatant sexism. If I was the son he'd wanted, he would've handed the partnership to me years ago on a golden platter. But, no, I'm just a frivolous, empty-headed girl like his three ex-wives. What would I know about advertising?'

'You know heaps,' Ivy reassured her. 'That dog food commercial you worked on last month was absolutely brilliant. And, if your mum was still alive, I know she would be proud of you.'

Zoey twisted her mouth and picked up her coffee cup again. 'Maybe, but I still lost the pitch to one of our biggest competitors. But I'm determined to win next time we're vying for the same account.' Her eyes began to sparkle with determination. 'I can't wait to wipe that arrogant smirk of victory off Finn McConnell's face once and for all.'

'You go, girl,' Ivy said, holding her coffee mug up in a toast. 'To achieving our goals—no matter what.'

Louis was not normally a thank-God-it's-Friday person. Call him a hard-nosed workaholic, but the weekends were when he got a sense of satisfaction from ticking off the long list of jobs he had to do that couldn't be done during the week. He often preferred to work at weekends rather than socialise, especially since his last lover had had trouble accepting he wasn't interested in taking things further than a short fling. But, as the weekend approached, he found himself thinking less about work and more about his 'date' with Ivy.

It was faintly disturbing how *much* he was thinking about her. Hardly an hour went by without him recalling the taste and velvety texture of her mouth. And he'd developed a sudden craving for strawberries. Every time he thought of what she'd asked him to do, he got aroused. He was distracted, daydreaming when he should have been working, mentally dwelling on what it would feel like to bury himself deep inside her and take them both to heaven.

But, while he could allow himself the odd daydream, what he couldn't allow was making those daydreams a reality. Ivy wasn't a one-night-stand type of woman and he'd had nothing but one-night stands. How could doing the deed with her be a good thing?

Louis had hours before he had to pick up Ivy, so he sat at his desk and worked on a project that needed some final adjustments before it was sent to the builder. His mind kept drifting to his date with Ivy. He blinked, sat up straighter in his chair and locked his gaze back on the design on the screen.

Work. Work. Work. He chanted the words to himself, but it wasn't long before his mind was going off on another tangent.

The possibility of sex.

A hot tingle ran down his spine and he shifted in his chair, cleared his throat and spoke out loud just to drive the point home.

'You can do this. You work ten to twelve hours a day. Get on with it.'

So now he was talking to himself as well as daydreaming about Ivy. He was well aware of the risk of spending more and more time with her. It might raise her expectations that he would solve her virginity problem. And he hadn't signed up for that—only the possibility of it which, weirdly, was making it even harder to resist her.

But he refused to think any further than spending the evening with her to help her feel more at ease. He was good at cordoning off his emotions, especially when it came to sex. Sex was a physical experience he enjoyed, like any other full-blooded man. He didn't associate any feelings with sex other than that of lust and pleasure. He had never been in love and never intended to be. He wasn't even sure the concept existed outside of novels and Hollywood movies. The chances of finding one person who complemented and fulfilled you in every way and would continue to do so throughout a lifetime was a fantasy in itself.

And one he *never* dabbled in.

But taking Ivy out a few times to help her build her confidence was certainly doable. There was no harm in kissing and fooling around a bit. No harm in that at all. His conscience rolled about the floor laughing.

Ahem. Mr Amazing One-Night Stand is going on a few dates with the same woman with only the possibility *of having sex? The man who doesn't date anyone longer than a day, and then only for sex?*

Louis leaned one elbow on his desk, pinched the bridge of his nose and tried to block the taunting of his conscience. He was thinking of Ivy, not himself.

She needed to be more relaxed without the pressure of sex hanging over her. That was his plan and it was a good one. A safe one. To hang out together on a few dates without the expectation of intimacy. Easy.

Louis continued to stare blankly at his computer, but then his phone suddenly rang and Ivy's number and name popped up on the screen. A stone landed in his gut with a sickening, organ-crushing thud. What if she was calling to cancel? What if she had changed her mind because he hadn't committed to her request? What if she'd decided to go with the stranger plan instead? Maybe someone else had already volunteered to take her virginity. Maybe she'd done it last night with a stranger she'd found online or even one of those male escort services.

He was ambushed by the host of unfamiliar emotions assailing him—disappointment right at the top of the list. He hadn't realised how much he was looking forward to being with her tonight until the possibility of it being cancelled became possible. She'd cancelled lunch a couple of months ago, and even now he didn't like admitting how disappointed he had been.

He snatched up his phone and answered it. 'Ivy.' He was pleased with how cool and collected he sounded when his heart was thumping as though he'd just consumed three energy drinks.

'Hiya, Louis, I just wanted to know what type of

clothes to wear. You didn't say where we were going tonight. Do I need to dress in anything fancy?'

He hadn't said because he hadn't decided until that morning. But he'd managed to secure box-seat tickets to a popular musical he knew she'd always wanted to see. He wanted their 'date' to be special and memorable. There was a risk of drawing press attention by being in such a public place. While he'd thought of taking her to his house in Chelsea or his place in the Cotswolds to afford them more privacy, he knew it wouldn't be wise to spend time completely alone with her. Tempting, yes, but definitely not wise. 'I've booked tickets to a West End musical. We can have supper afterwards.'

'Oh, what fun! I haven't been to the West End in ages. Shall I meet you there or—?'

'Ivy, when I date a woman I pick her up and I take her home. I'll see you at seven.'

Ivy was putting the last touches to her make-up when the doorbell sounded, announcing Louis' arrival. She pressed her lips together to set her lipgloss, quickly snatched up her evening bag and went out of her bedroom to greet him. When she saw him standing there in a dark charcoal suit, with a crisp white shirt and blue-and-grey-striped tie, her breath caught and her heart did a funny little skip. He was the epitome of a handsome, successful male in his prime.

'Hiya. Do you want to come in for a minute? No one else is home.'

'Sure.' He stepped over the threshold and she closed the door.

Suddenly her flat seemed too small to accommodate his six-foot-four frame. She could smell the citrus and woodsy notes of his aftershave and his eyes looked darker than normal—more pupil than iris. His gaze swept over her black cocktail dress and high heels and then back to her face.

'You look stunning.' His voice had a rusty edge that did strange swoopy things to her stomach.

Ivy smoothed her hands down her hips. 'I bought it this afternoon. I thought I'd better treat myself since this is my first proper date in months.'

'How many months?'

She could feel her cheeks warming and leaned down to pick up her bag from where she'd put it when she'd answered the door. 'Ten.' She cast him a sideways glance. 'I've been out with girlfriends and stuff but not alone with a guy for close to a year.' She twisted her mouth in a rueful grimace. 'Kind of weird for an almost-thirty-year-old, huh?'

He came over to her and took one of her hands in his, stroking his thumb over the back of her hand, his eyes locking on hers. 'It's a little unusual but definitely not weird.' He gave her hand a light squeeze and released it, slipping his hand in his suit pocket as if determined not to touch her.

Ivy was aware of the grey-blue intensity of his gaze, aware of the tightening of the air, aware of the faint tingling of her skin where his thumb had stroked. 'So, how was your day?' Nothing like a bit of inane conversation to recalibrate the atmosphere.

Louis glanced at her mouth and her stomach swooped and dived again. 'Boring until now.'

She moistened her lips, her pulse fluttering. 'Are you flirting with me?'

He stepped closer, his hands taking both of hers, his thumbs doing the spine-loosening, stroking motion again. 'Isn't that what a man does when he takes a woman out on a date?'

Ivy's stomach fluttered and she couldn't stop staring at his mouth. 'If I was one of your normal dates, you would sleep with me at the end of the evening, wouldn't you? How do I know if you will or you won't?'

His eyes moved between each of hers—back and forth, back and forth—each time making her heart beat a little faster. Then they dipped to her mouth and he slid a hand along the side of her face until his fingers were entangled in her hair. 'It's always a possibility, but let's wait and see.' His tone contained a relaxed go-with-the-flow note but his eyes communicated something else. The flared pupils, the concentrated focus, all spoke of a man who was tempted, seriously tempted, to act on his primal desires.

Ivy didn't know whether to be relieved or disappointed. She was stuck in a strangely exciting limbo of 'would he or wouldn't he?'. She began to step back, but before she could take even half a step he caught her by the wrist, his fingers overlapping.

'It's not that I don't want to, *ma petite.*' His voice had dropped even lower in pitch and it sent a wave of goose bumps tiptoeing over her skin. He brought her wrist up to his mouth and pressed a kiss to her leaping pulse, his eyes holding hers. 'I've been thinking about little else all day.'

Ivy swallowed. 'Really?'

He gave a rueful slant of a smile. 'Really.' He released her wrist and stepped back to open the door. 'We'd better get going. They won't let us in until after the interval if we show up late.'

Ivy followed him out of her flat to where he had parked his car half a block up the road. He helped her into the passenger seat and pulled down the seatbelt for her. She clipped it into place and watched as he strode around to his side of the car, the lines and planes of his face so familiar and yet so strange. It was as if she were seeing him for the first time, not as her older brother's friend but as a virile thirty-four-year-old man with primal drives and desires. A man who was attracted to her and, unless she was very much mistaken, tempted to do as she asked. A tiny frisson passed over her flesh and her breath hitched at the thought of him being her first lover. Maybe even tonight.

Louis slipped into the driver's seat beside her and sent her a glance. 'Relax, *ma petite*. We're just hanging out together to see what happens. Okay?'

Ivy could feel a blush rising to the roots of her hair. 'How did you know what I was thinking?'

He gave a slow smile and started the engine with a throaty roar. 'Because I'm thinking it myself.'

He backed out of the parking space and deftly wove into the traffic, and for once in her life Ivy was lost for words.

Musicals weren't really Louis' thing, but he enjoyed watching Ivy being captivated by the songs, the costumes and stage set of the popular musical. She looked captivating herself in a dress that hugged her breasts and thighs, her impossibly high heels showcasing her legs and ankles. Every now and again he caught a whiff of her flowery perfume and, every time she glanced his way with her shining gaze, his heart would trip like a foot missing a step on a ladder.

The theatre was packed, and he was dreading being noticed, but it was worth it to see Ivy having such a good time. During the interval, once they had their drinks with them in the private box, she leaned closer to point out something in the programme he'd bought her. 'Hey, isn't that the actor in that BBC drama you recommended a few months ago?'

Louis looked at the name and nodded. 'Yep. That's her.'

'Did you ever date her?'

'No.'

Ivy swept her gaze over the audience below. 'On balance, given you've slept with so many women, there must be a few of your past lovers here, don't you think?'

'It's highly unlikely.'

'Why's that?'

He turned his head to look at her. 'The press grossly overstates my sexual proclivity. If I'd slept with as many women as reported, I'd never have been able to build such a success of my career.'

'Why are you driven to work so hard? Ronan told me you hardly ever take holidays and you often work weekends and public holidays.'

Louis leaned back in his seat and picked up his glass of champagne from the holder on his seat. 'I run an architectural business. I have people depending on me, clients and staff, and I'm committed to doing a good job of everything I take on.' He took a sip of champagne, savouring the pear and honey notes.

'Do you enjoy it?'

'Of course I enjoy it.' He put down his glass and glanced at his watch to see how much longer before the second half of the show. 'It sure beats the hell out of being an accountant.'

'Is that what your father wanted? For you to work in his accountancy firm?'

Louis was conscious of his jaw automatically tightening. 'In my father's mind, I let the family line down by pursuing architecture instead of accountancy like him and his father before him. The Charpentier accountancy firm will end with my father and for that he will never forgive me. Nor, I suspect, will my mother, mostly because she desperately wants grandchildren and I'm not interested in providing them.'

He picked up his champagne again and took another sip. That was another feeling he suppressed—the guilt he felt about his mother's hopes and dreams being dashed by his decision.

Ivy's small white teeth sank into the pillow-softness of her lower lip and her eyes lost their sparkle. 'Oh, Louis, that's terrible. You have to live your own life—fulfil your own dreams and aspirations instead of those of your parents'.'

'Try telling them that.' Louis gave a twisted smile and put his champagne glass down again before he spilled any more family secrets.

'Maybe you'll change your mind about having kids one day,' Ivy said after a small silence. 'Lots of men do. Even Ronan is considering having a child

with Ricky via a surrogate. He'll be a great dad, and
so would you if you'd—'

'I won't change my mind.'

Just then the bell rang to announce the end of
the interval and people started filing back into the
theatre.

Louis was relieved the conversation was halted
by the bell. He rarely spoke to anyone about his family. Not out of a sense of disloyalty to his parents but
rather because it was nothing short of depressing to
know how much of a disappointment he was to his
family. The strange thing was, his grandfather had
been exactly like his father—nit-picking, pedantic
and overly critical of anyone who didn't follow his
orders to a T. Another good reason for Louis to resist the biological drive to procreate. The last thing
the world needed was another difficult Charpentier.

Ivy left the theatre with Louis after the musical
came to an end. She had enjoyed it immensely but
found she could barely recall what'd happened in the
second half because she'd been mulling over what
Louis had told her about his family. And his adamant stance on never having children. Even though
she knew it was none of her business what choices
he made about his life, a part of her felt sad he would
never experience the joys of parenthood, not to mention the satisfaction of a long-term relationship with
a partner. He said he had never fallen in love, but

she wondered if he would never allow himself to, closing off his emotions so he wasn't made vulnerable by anyone. She, on the other hand, longed to be loved and supported by a lifelong partner, someone who wouldn't reject her or give up his love for her the way her father had done so easily.

Louis led her to a wine bar that served cocktails and light meals, a short walk from the theatre. Their table was upstairs in an exclusive and private section that overlooked the bustling street below.

Ivy sat on the plush velvet wing-back chair opposite Louis and looked around the room with avid appreciation. 'This is gorgeous. I've never been here before. I feel like royalty or a celebrity or something.'

'A friend I went to university with owns it,' Louis said, handing her the cocktail menu. 'What would you like to drink?'

Ivy looked at the array of exotic cocktails. 'Let me see, now… Gosh, so many to choose from. What do you recommend?'

'How about a strawberry gin cocktail?' He pointed to the one on the menu.

'Sounds good. I love strawberries.'

His eyes flicked to her lips and one side of his mouth curved upwards. 'I've developed rather a fancy for them myself lately.'

Something about his wry tone sent a light shiver over her skin.

Their drinks soon appeared, and soon after that a light tapas-style supper followed, with a host of flavoursome delicacies both savoury and sweet. Once she had eaten her fill, Ivy dabbed at the corners of her mouth with her linen napkin and, setting it aside, sat back in her chair. 'That was amazing. Thank you for taking me out tonight. I've had the best time.'

'My pleasure. I enjoyed it too.'

She twisted her mouth. 'You don't seem like the West End musical type. I thought you'd rather go to a classical symphony concert.'

Louis shrugged one broad shoulder and then leaned forward to pick up his cocktail. 'You're making me sound staid and boring.'

'You're definitely not that.'

His eyes locked on hers and a faint prickly sensation ran down her spine and down the back of her legs. She ran the tip of her tongue over her lips and drew in a wobbly breath. Either that strawberry gin cocktail was going to her head or Louis was making her feel things she had never felt before. The energy in the air shifted, a subtle tightening, as if all the oxygen particles had been disturbed.

A band was playing in the background and Louis leaned forward to put his cocktail back on the table. He pushed back his chair and stood, offering his hand to her. 'Would you like to dance?'

'Sure. Why not?' Ivy took his proffered hand and went with him to the small dance floor. They moved in perfect time to the sweetly cadenced ballad, and she was conscious of every point of contact with him. One of his arms was around her, his other hand holding hers, her cheek resting on his chest right where his heart beat so steadily. Her heart was doing an Irish jig in her chest, and when he tipped up her face to meet his gaze it did a backflip.

His arm around her tightened just enough to bring her closer to the heat of his pelvis, his mouth slowly, ever so slowly, coming down to hers. His lips were warm and gentle, but then his pressure increased, sending shooting sparks of pleasure through her body. His tongue stroked for entry—a lazy let-me-play-with-you stroke that sent a lightning bolt of lust straight to her core. She suddenly remembered they were in a public place, on a dance floor surrounded by other people, and she pulled back, biting her lip where his tempting tongue had just been. 'Sorry. A bit public for me.'

He gave both her hands a squeeze and smiled. 'You're right. Now is not the time or place.' He led her back to the table and they each took their seats.

Ivy aimed her attention at his mouth rather than hold his gaze. 'But when and where will be the time and place?' He didn't answer for so long, she brought her gaze up to meet his.

His expression was difficult to read, but somehow she sensed he had come to a decision in his mind. 'What are you doing next Friday night?'

'I haven't got anything planned. Why?'

'I have a place down in the Cotswolds. I thought we could spend the night there and drive back on Saturday morning.'

Ivy blinked. 'Does that mean you're going to…?'

'You have a one-track mind.' His tone was playfully reproving. 'No, it doesn't necessarily mean we're going to sleep together.'

'But what is the point of us hanging out together if you don't do what I asked you to do? I've only got three weeks now until my birthday. Time is rapidly running out.'

'Why the big hurry to do it before your birthday?'

She opened her eyes wide. 'Why the hurry? Because I made a promise to myself that I wouldn't still be a virgin by then. If you're not going to help me, say so, Louis. It's not fair to string me along if you've no intention of—'

'I would do it in a heartbeat if I was confident we both wouldn't regret it in the end.'

'You know what I think?' Ivy shot him a heated glare. 'I think you're the one who's worried about getting hurt in the end. You spend your life sleeping only once with women you'll never see again because you're worried about feeling something for someone.' She snatched up her bag from the table. 'Thank you for this evening. I'll make my own way home. And I'll find someone else to help me, so you're off the hook. Goodbye.'

'Ivy.' His voice had a commanding note. 'Wait.'

She turned from the door to face him. 'I've wasted enough time waiting. I get it. You don't want to help me. You're not attracted to me even though you give a very good impression of it. But I'm a big girl. I can handle the rejection. God knows, I've had plenty of practice.'

He came over to her and took both her hands in his. A battle played out on his features, a war of conflicting emotions he was clearly trying to hide, but she could see it in the shadows in his eyes and the tightness in his jaw and the thinning of his lips. 'Okay. Here's the deal. One night and one night only. I'll pick you up on Friday after work. And on Saturday we go back to being friends as normal.'

Ivy wanted to refuse his offer out of pride but the thought of anyone else sleeping with her turned her stomach. It *had* to be him. 'Okay.'

He gave her hands a quick squeeze and then tucked one of her arms through his. 'Come on, Cinderella. Time to get you home.'

Louis spent the following week wondering if he needed his head read for agreeing to Ivy's plan. He'd been at war with himself from the moment she'd put it to him. He'd been dragging his heels, not so much because he didn't want to do it but because he did. Badly. The more time he spent with her, the more he wanted her.

Normally his week at work flew past but this one dragged as if someone had slowed down time. He had deliberately delayed going down to the Cotswolds for another week to give her a cooling-off period. Didn't all good business deals involve a cooling-off period? And the only way to approach her plan was to keep things businesslike. One night was all she wanted. One night was all he ever gave. But Louis became so restless and on edge, he finally caved in and called Ivy on her mobile just after two on the Friday.

'What time will you be ready? A client cancelled a meeting, so we can go earlier to get ahead of the traffic.' It wasn't exactly a lie—a client had cancelled, but it had been earlier that morning. Louis had plenty of work he could have seen to if he'd wanted to but he couldn't wait to whisk Ivy away to his own private little paradise.

'I'll be ready in half an hour.'

'Perfect. See you soon.' Louis clicked off his phone and took a deep, steadying breath. If his secretary, Natalie, could have seen him now—leaving work in the middle of the afternoon and taking most of the weekend off—she would have raised her brows until they disappeared under her fringe, or reached for a thermometer and threatened to call a doctor. He smiled and pushed back his chair to stand, grabbing his keys and phone off the desk.

For once, work could wait.

CHAPTER FOUR

Ivy wasn't the best packer on the planet for an overnighter. All the weekend access visits to her father after her parents had divorced during her teens had ramped up her anxiety to the point where now she couldn't pack a bag without worrying about all the things she might need, so she took everything just in case. Her bedroom looked as if it had been done over by a burglar. Her wardrobe had turned into a 'floordrobe' and she couldn't find the matching knickers to her favourite black bra.

Why hadn't she bought some new underwear? What if Louis was turned off by her lingerie? But there was a new level of anxiety in packing this particular bag. She was actually going to do it.

She was going to have sex. With Louis.

The doorbell sounded and her stomach dropped. He was here and she wasn't properly prepared. The day was finally here and she was stuffing around, trying to decide what underwear to take. She went to the front door and opened it, her heart doing a funny little hopscotch when she laid eyes on Louis, still dressed in his business wear, although he'd removed his tie.

'I'm almost ready. Do you want to sit down while I finish packing? Or shall I make you a coffee or something? A juice or—?'

'Don't be nervous, *ma petite.*' His husky tone almost made her swoon, so too the look of concern in his eyes.

Ivy could feel a blush stealing over her cheeks. 'I'm sorry to be so flustered. I'm just hopeless at packing. I always take too much stuff and then end up without the things I most need.'

He gave one of his slanted smiles and her heart tripped again. 'You look good in anything you wear.'

A pool of heat swirled in her lower body and her pulse went off the charts. 'So do you.'

A twinkle came into his eyes. 'Are you flirting with me?'

She gave him a coy smile. 'I think I might be.'

He stepped across the threshold and closed the door, taking her by the upper arms and bringing her close to his body. His eyes darkened and became hooded, his head bending down so his mouth was just above hers.

'I told myself I wouldn't do this, but I've been thinking about nothing else for days.' He closed the distance between their mouths in a kiss that threatened to blow the top of her head off. Desire flared and ran like hot flames through her body. His tongue entered her mouth on a silken thrust that had distinctly erotic undertones and she shivered in delight. His hands moved from her upper arms and went around her body, drawing her closer to his hard frame. She could feel the thickening of his body, the signal of his arousal, and another wave of incendiary heat swept through her. One of his hands came up to cradle the back of her head, his fingers splaying through her hair. He groaned against her mouth, a deep, guttural sound that sent a shudder of need right through her body. It was beyond thrilling to hear and feel his response to her. It made her confidence grow, like a plant starved of water finally receiving a life-saving drink.

Louis eased back to look down at her. 'Are you still sure about this?'

Ivy was getting off just being held in his arms. Never had her body felt so warm and tingly, especially with his erection pressing against her feminine mound. Why wasn't she freaking out and trying to put some distance between them? Or was it because Louis' body spoke to hers in a way that made her feel more confident in her sensuality? 'Yes. It feels like you are too.'

His pupils flared like black holes in infinite space. 'I've thinking about nothing else all week.'

Ivy could feel heat stealing over her cheeks. 'I hope

I'm not a disappointment. I'm such a prude, I can't even watch sex scenes in movies without blushing.'

He stroked a gentle finger down the curve of her hot cheek. 'I think it's cute how you blush all the time. Don't ever apologise for it.' The timbre of his voice made her legs feel weak. Or maybe it was the tender look in his eyes.

Ivy patted his chest with one of her hands. 'I'm holding us up. Give me five minutes to finish packing?'

He bent down and brushed her lips with his. 'Go for it.'

Louis had to stop himself from following her into her bedroom and finishing what he'd started. Yes. What *he'd* started. So much for his boundaries. He'd promised himself he would keep his hands off her until they got to his place in the country, yet as soon as he'd seen her he'd crushed his mouth on hers like a magnet attracted to metal.

He scraped a hand through his hair, trying to get his breathing back under control. Every time he kissed her, it made him want her all the more. It was as though a switch inside him had been flicked and there was no turning it off again. Kissing her at the wine bar had nailed it for him. A kiss here or there was never going to cut it. Not now. He was too far gone for that. He wanted her with a fervour that was unlike anything he had felt before.

Desire pounded through him with an unstoppable

force, a need so raw and primal he felt it in every cell of his body. He wanted to think it was because he hadn't had sex in four months but, deep down, he suspected it was more to do with Ivy. She was some-one he cared about, someone he respected, someone he would continue to see long after their physical relationship ended. It made their alliance dangerous in a way none of his previous encounters had been. But he was a master at putting emotions to one side when he needed to. This would be no different. Their little secret tryst in the country had all the makings of a hot-blooded fantasy. *If* he allowed it.

The thought wandered about his mind like a stray guest in a mansion looking at things he shouldn't be looking at, touching things he shouldn't touch. Tres-passing into areas he had never allowed himself to go before. They would be spending the night doing all the things he'd told himself they weren't going to do…

Louis pulled himself out of his reverie and wan-dered over to the sideboard in the sitting room where a group of photos was displayed. There was one of Ivy and Ronan at his graduation, another of Ivy with two attractive young women he presumed were her current flatmates. His gaze landed on another one of Ivy as a child at an Irish dancing contest. He picked up the photo frame and couldn't hold back a smile. The red-gold-haired cherub in that photo was enough to make anyone's heart melt.

He put the photo down and his gaze went to the one of her rescue dog, Fergus, who had died a couple of years ago. Ronan had told him Ivy had been inconsolable and on an impulse Louis had sent her flowers and a card. She'd sent him a neatly written thank-you note that he still had in his filing cabinet. He couldn't quite explain why he'd kept it.

Ivy came back into the sitting room lugging two overnight bags. 'I'm ready.'

'Here, let me take those for you,' Louis said, reaching for them. 'What have you got in them? A full set of encyclopaedias?'

Her cheeks pooled with twin circles of pink. 'I hate people who can go away for a weekend and fit everything in one bag. My make-up and toiletries fill one bag on their own.'

Louis gave a soft laugh. 'Come on. Let's get going before we get stuck in traffic.'

He wanted no time wasted until he could kiss her again.

About two hours after leaving London, and after driving down a long, winding hawthorn-fringed lane and over a narrow bridge across a small river, they arrived at a traditional Cotswold-stone manor house. Ivy leaned forward in her seat in excitement, struck by the beauty of the gardens surrounding the house that had been recently renovated, with an extension that perfectly suited the old bones of

the house. 'You said it was a little place in the Cotswolds. This is huge!'

'Only ten bedrooms,' Louis said. 'I could have
bought one with fifteen but thought that was a little
over the top for one person.'

She glanced at him as he brought the car to a halt
in front of the house. 'But don't you want to have
a family one day to share this with? I mean, this
would be ideal for—'

'No.' His tone was blunt. Emphatic. Decision
made and will not be changed. 'I don't.'

Ivy unclipped her seatbelt, more than a little intrigued as to why he was so adamant against settling
down one day. 'How often do you come down here?'

'Not often enough.' He got out of the car and
came around to her side to help her out. 'I have a
caretaker and housekeeper and a couple of garden-
ers who keep things in check. I try to spend a couple of weeks here in the summer and the occasional
weekend throughout the year.'

'Is that all?' She looked at him in surprise. 'If
this was my place, I would never want to leave. It's
so private and peaceful.'

'Speaking of private—we're keeping our time
together a secret, right? I don't want anyone spec-
ulating that we're an item. The press would have a
field day.'

'Sure…' Ivy avoided his gaze, pretending an avid

interest in a garden sculpture near the front of the house.

'Ivy.' His tone was commanding. 'Look at me.'

She sucked her lower lip inside her mouth and turned to glance at him. His gaze was probing, the line of his mouth firm. 'I'm sorry, I wasn't going to tell Millie, but then…but it kind of slipped out the other week when we first went out for dinner, and then she told Zoey.'

'Oh, God.' His despairing groan was a shattering blow to her self-esteem. Was it so embarrassing for him to be associated with her, even for a weekend? 'And who else will they tell? Will it be all over social media by now?'

'Don't be ridiculous, they would never do something like that.'

'Who else have you told? Your mother? Or Ronan?' His frown was savage, his eyes as piercing as a detective honing in on a suspect.

'No, of course not.' Ivy sent him a glowering look. 'Do you really think I'd crow to all and sundry that you're helping me with my intimacy issues? It's embarrassing enough for me without broadcasting it to the world.'

He released a rough sigh that had a note of resignation on its backdraft and turned to pop the boot open. 'Okay. Fine. But don't tell anyone else.'

She looked down at her feet and kicked at a pebble with her toe. 'Is this embarrassing for you too?

I mean, being here with me?' She somehow found the courage to meet his gaze once more.

His expression was unreadable. 'No. Not at all.' He turned and took her bags out of the boot as if they weighed nothing more than a couple of pillows. 'Come on. I'll show you round.'

Ivy breathed in the scents from the herbaceous border—stocks and lupins and foxgloves and hollyhocks, the colourful array attracting busy bees and fluttering butterflies. The early-summer sunshine was surprisingly warm and was a stark contrast to the greyness of the London sky they had left behind close to two hours ago. Birds twittered in the shrubbery and the neatly trimmed hedges, and in the distance, she heard the eerie call of a peacock on a neighbouring property. She followed Louis to the front entrance of the grand manor house, wondering how many other women he had brought here. Should she ask or would it seem too intrusive?

He put down her bags, deactivated the alarm system on his key fob and unlocked the front door, pushing it open for her. 'In you go. I'll take these up to your room and then come and show you around.'

'Why separate rooms? Aren't we supposed to be—?'

'I'm a restless sleeper, and I often get up to work at night. Besides, you won't be up to marathon sessions just yet.'

Ivy stepped into the house and turned to face him once he'd brought the bags in and closed the door. 'How many women have you brought here for marathon sessions? Or have you lost count?'

He placed his keys in a glass bowl on a polished hall table—a beautiful Regency piece that was in perfect condition. 'I've never brought anyone here before.'

She raised her eyebrows. 'Really? Why not?'

'I come down here to chill out and relax. I find relationships—even temporary ones—hard work.'

Ivy shifted her gaze, her teeth savaging her lip. 'I hope my presence isn't going to spoil your precious idyll for you.'

He stepped forward and trailed his index finger down her cheek, his expression softening. 'It won't. I'd thought of asking you and Ronan down some time anyway. I just didn't get round to it before he emigrated to Australia because the renovations took a little longer than I expected.'

Ivy was conscious of her heartbeat increasing at his proximity. Aware of the tingle in her cheek from his faineant touch. Her gaze drifted to his mouth and something in her stomach fell off a shelf with a soft little *kerplunk*. His jaw was peppered with late-in-the-day stubble and, before she could stop herself, she lifted her hand to his face and stroked it down the sexy prickles, the sound overly loud in the silence. 'Thanks for bringing me here. It's so beautiful and I already feel relaxed.'

His hand came up and encircled her wrist, and for a moment she thought he was going to remove her hand from his face and set her away from him. But then his eyes darkened and he brought her inexorably closer, until she was flush against his rock-hard body. She smothered a gasp, her heart thumping so loudly she wondered if he could feel it pounding against his chest.

'I have this insatiable desire to kiss you.' His voice was so deep and rough, it made her skin lift in a delicious shiver.

'Same here.' Her voice was barely more than a hoarse whisper.

His eyes went to her mouth and he muttered a swear word and brought his down to hers. It was a kiss of fervent passion that made every hair on her head lift off her scalp. Desire flooded her being, giant waves of it coursing through her body in scorching-hot streaks. His hands skated down the sides of her body and then settled on her hips, bringing her even closer to the jutting heat of his. He lifted his mouth off hers, his eyes glittering with unbridled lust. 'I'm finding it hard to believe you need any tutoring from me. You turn me on so much I can barely stand it.'

Ivy glowed at his compliment and her damaged ego crawled out of the corner and unfolded itself from the foetal position. 'I didn't realise it would be this way between us.' She stroked his lean jaw again. 'But I'm worried you'll be disappointed when it comes to having sex with me.'

His eyes darkened to a midnight-blue. 'You won't disappoint me.' He brushed the pad of his thumb over her lip where her teeth had just been. 'Now, let's get you unpacked, and we'll have a drink in the garden before dinner.'

Ivy followed him up the stairs with her body still buzzing from his passionate kiss. If she'd had the confidence, she'd have insisted he make love to her right now. Why wait when they were alone for the whole weekend?

But maybe he was right not to rush her. She needed to take things slowly, to be more in control of what happened with her body. Her previous dates had pressured her, and it had made her panic, and they hadn't taken the rejection well. One had made insulting comments about her body that she had been fretting over ever since. She wanted it to be different this time. To be able to enjoy every moment without embarrassment, or feeling pressured and on edge, or fearful of being body shamed.

Louis led her to a room on the second storey that had a beautiful view of the back garden and the rolling fields beyond the estate. Her bedroom was decorated in cream and white, which gave the room a spacious and luxurious feel that would rival that of any top hotel. Her eyes went to the queen-sized bed and molten heat pooled between her legs at the thought of lying in it with Louis, his body buried deeply in hers...

He placed the bags on a velvet-covered linen box at the end of the bed and straightened to look at her. 'There's an *en suite* bathroom through there.'

'Where's your room?'

'Further down the hall.'

'How much further?'

He released a heavy sigh and reached to tuck a loose strand of her hair back behind her ear. 'Don't take it personally. I often get up at night and tinker away on my computer. I wouldn't want to disturb you.'

Ivy searched his features for a crack in the firewall of his self-control. He kept glancing at her mouth as if unable to pull his gaze away. And there was a doggedness about the line of his jaw, as if he was calling on every bit of willpower to stop himself from acting on the desire she could see shining in his eyes. 'You work too hard.'

He gave a lop-sided smile and released her. 'I'm going to rustle up some dinner. Come down when you're ready.'

Louis left her to unpack and went downstairs to check if his housekeeper had followed his instructions to leave supplies for dinner. Yep. Done, and done well. Who said you couldn't get good help these days?

The dining room was set up, the fridge and pantry stocked, the champagne and wine on chill. A casserole was in the slow cooker, filling the kitchen with the fragrant aroma of chicken and herbs. There were even flowers from the garden on the table and throughout the house, filling the air with a summery smell.

The garden was bathed in golden early-evening sunlight, making him wonder why he didn't come down here more often to relax. Like 'commitment', 'relax' was another word he'd shied away from in his quest to succeed as an architect. The thing was, he now had the success he'd always aimed for, but he still kept striving. He was stuck in work gear, always going at full throttle, because that was all he knew now. It was all he wanted, right? Work. Achievement. Success.

Louis opened the fridge and took out the champagne. He got two glasses from the cabinet and placed them on a tray, along with cheese, crackers, fruit and pâté. He heard Ivy's footsteps coming down the stairs and along the passage to the kitchen and something deep and low in his pelvis tightened. *Sheesh.* Even the sound of her footsteps got his blood roaring.

She came into the kitchen wearing a long, summery, Bohemian-style off-the-shoulder dress that highlighted the creamy perfection of her neck and shoulders. Her hair was bundled up in a makeshift up-do with some loose tendrils cascading about her heart-shaped face. She glanced at the champagne and smiled, making her eyes sparkle. 'That's my favourite.'

'I know.' Louis picked up the tray and nodded towards the French doors leading to the garden. 'Let's take this outside and enjoy the sunlight before dinner.'

Ivy walked ahead of him and opened the door, then followed him out to the garden. 'I love your garden. Was it already like this or did you design it?'

'I made some changes, along with the house.'

Louis put the tray down on the outdoor table under the wisteria trellis, the sweet fragrance of the pendulous blooms as heady as a drug. Or maybe he was feeling a little intoxicated by the way Ivy looked and the fact she was here. Alone with him.

'How long have you had this place?'

'Three years.' He uncorked the bottle and poured out two glasses. He put the bottle down, handed her a glass then picked up his own.

Ivy took the glass from him, her fingers brushing his, and a jolt of electricity shot through him. 'I really like the way you've blended the old with the new. You didn't think of designing a new house from scratch like you do for most of your clients?'

Louis shrugged one shoulder. 'I saw this place and liked it. It had good bones, so I didn't see the sense in changing it too much, just enough to put my stamp on it.'

'I think you've done an amazing job,' she said, turning back to look at the house. Now that her back was towards him, Louis had an uncontrollable urge to press a kiss to the back of her neck where red-gold curls dangled like miniature corkscrews.

She turned around again and smiled. 'Your parents must be so proud of you. How many awards have you won now? Dozens?'

Louis held his glass to hers. 'To achieving goals.'

Her brow furrowed, her blue eyes searching his. 'They *are* proud of you, aren't they? I mean, you're one of the most talented architects in the world. Ronan told me you have a long waiting list of clients desperate for you to work for them.'

'I don't like talking about my family. It's too depressing to be reminded of how much of a disappointment I am to them, especially to my father.' He handed her the plate of cheese and fruit. 'Want some?'

She took a grape off the plate and popped it in her mouth. After she'd swallowed it, she took a portion of cheese and placed it on a cracker. 'I'm glad my parents never really interfered with Ronan's or my career plans. I love working in antiques and can't imagine doing anything else.'

'What do you love about it?'

'So many things…like the fact that generations of people have used a piece of furniture or crockery, or glassware or jewellery, before. The sense of history fascinates me.' Her face shone with enthusiasm, her tone almost reverent as she went on. 'My pet love is Victorian crockery. I sometimes just hold a piece of it in my hand and imagine the people who have used it before. I'm going to Paris next week to see a collection from a deceased estate.'

Louis reached out and tucked one of her loose tendrils behind her ear. 'It's not ridiculous to be passionate about something.'

Her eyes dipped to his mouth and back again, the tip of her tongue darting out to moisten her lips. A rocket blast of lust hit him like a sucker punch, and he took the champagne glass off her and set it down beside his on the table. He took her hands in his and brought her closer to his body. 'And while we're on the topic of passion…'

He lowered his mouth to her upturned one, her lips flowering open to the gentle pressure of his. She made a soft whimpering sound and rose up on tiptoe, her hands creeping up to link around his neck, the action bringing her even closer. Dangerously, temptingly, tantalisingly closer. He entered her mouth with a bold stroke of his tongue, shivers coursing down his spine as her tongue mated shyly with his. The playful little darts and flickers of her tongue sent his pulse soaring, the delicious press of her breasts against his chest making him wild with primal want. Heat poured into his lower body—hot, hard heat that threatened to engulf him.

Louis placed a hand at the small of her back, just above the sweet curve of her bottom, his senses reeling at the way her mouth responded to him with such passionate fervour. He brought his other hand to the curve of her breast, cradling it through her dress, allowing her time to get used to being touched so intimately. She made another sound of encouragement and leaned her pelvis further into him, moving against him in an instinctive fashion. He lifted his mouth off hers and placed it on the exquisite softness of her neck, trailing slow kisses from below her ear, over her shoulder and to the upper curve of her breasts. She drew in a hitching breath, gasping in pleasure, and he stroked his tongue over the exposed part of her breast, aching to explore her in more intimate detail. He began gently to tug her dress down to reveal more of her breast, but she suddenly froze and then pushed his hand away.

'I'm sorry…' She bit her lip, her cheeks bright pink.

Louis placed his hands on her hips. 'Too soon for you?'

'It's not that…'

'What is it? Talk to me, Ivy. Tell me what's worrying you about me touching you like that.'

She swallowed and brought her gaze back to his. 'My breasts are small. I'm worried you won't find them attractive.'

He stroked a lazy finger down the curve of her blushing cheek. 'I find everything about you attractive.'

A tremulous smile flirted with the edges of her mouth, but the shadows hadn't gone from her eyes. 'One of the dates I had made a comment about my breasts when I told him I didn't want to sleep with him, and I've never really got over it. I can't look at my body without thinking how unappealing it must be to men.'

Louis had to suppress a wave of anger so intense it threatened to boil his blood at what that jerk of a boyfriend had said to her. 'Ivy, that idiot guy needs to be taught a lesson and I wish I could be the one to teach him. You have no reason to be ashamed of any part of your body. I've been trying not to notice for years how damn attractive you are.'

Ivy peered up into his face as if she couldn't quite believe what he'd said was true. 'Really? You never gave me any indication.'

He played with a loose curl of her hair, winding it around his finger and releasing it again. 'Yes, well, your brother might have had something to say about it if I had, knowing my playboy reputation with women.' He frowned and added, 'I can't help thinking he won't be too happy about us spending the night together. I promised to keep an eye on you, not to sleep with you.'

Ivy pursed her lips, eyes flashing. 'It's time my brother accepted I'm not a child any more. I want to sleep with you, Louis.' She took one of his hands and placed it back on her breast. 'Now, where were we?'

Louis smiled. 'Well, I was about to do this…' He gently peeled her dress down to uncover half of her bra-less breast and then lowered his mouth to the ripe curve. She gave a soft sound of approval and he pulled the dress a little lower to uncover her nipple. He rolled his tongue over and around her peaking flesh, delighting in the exquisite softness of her skin and the way she was responding to his caresses.

'Oh…oh…*oh*…' Her voice was a breathless thread of sound and she gave a little shudder.

Louis lifted his head to look at her, his hands going to her hips to steady her. 'Okay so far?'

Her eyes shimmered with the same desire he could feel thundering through his body. Hot. Urgent. Desperate. 'More than okay. It feels so good to have you touch me like that.' She sounded almost surprised that she enjoyed it. 'Do it again. Please?'

'Your wish is my command.' *And my most wicked fantasy.*

Louis bent his head and placed his mouth over her right breast, sucking softly, teasing her with his lips and tongue and the gentle tether of his teeth. Her skin was like silk and she smelled of flowers and vanilla and musk, sending his senses haywire. He moved his mouth to her other breast, exploring it in the same thorough detail, delighting in the sounds of encouragement she was making, thrilled by her avid response to his touch.

She quivered under his hands, her eyelashes at half-mast, as if drunk on the sensations he was triggering in her. Powerful, intense sensations that were erupting vicariously through his own flesh. His erection was so tight and heavy it was painful, the desire for completion a pounding primal force in his blood. But he needed to be in control and, right now, his control was slipping away, pushing every thought aside for the goal of intense physical satisfaction.

But this wasn't like any other one-nighter. This was Ivy and he had to take things slowly. Painfully, agonisingly slowly. With a strength of will he didn't know he still possessed, he eased back from her, breathing heavily. 'Let's take a breather. I said I wasn't going to rush you and I'm not going back on my word.'

Disappointment spread over her features, her cheeks darkening to a warm shade of pink. 'Did I do something wrong?' Worry was threaded through her voice and her teeth captured her lower lip.

Louis framed her face in his hands, holding her troubled gaze. 'You did nothing wrong, *ma chérie*. I want your first time to be perfect and making love out here in the open is probably not the way to do it.'

'So, you're not going to change your mind about making love with me?'

He brushed her mouth with a light kiss. 'If I were a better man, then perhaps I would.' He gave a rueful twist of his lips and added, 'You've done strange things to my moral compass.'

A small frown formed a tiny crease in the smooth perfection of her forehead. 'What's immoral about two consenting adults having sex? We're not doing anything wrong or illegal.'

'I know, but we'll only be having sex tonight,' Louis said, watching her steadily. 'I don't want there to be any confusion about that. This is not happening after we leave here tomorrow, okay?' He wasn't sure if he was saying it for her benefit or his. But it needed to be said. And underlined.

Her eyes drifted to his mouth and her tongue poked out to wet her lips. 'I understand the terms, Louis. You don't have to spell them out all the time. I only want this night with you. After that, we go back to being friends as normal.'

He had a feeling nothing would ever be normal again. He bent down and pressed another kiss to her soft mouth. 'Stay here and finish your drink and enjoy the garden while I sort out dinner.'

And get my self-control back in order.

CHAPTER FIVE

IVY WATCHED HIM go back into the house and wished she had the courage to go in after him to distract him from cooking dinner and make him take her straight upstairs to bed. But she knew he was determined to take things slowly and a part of her was grateful he wasn't rushing her. She had been rushed before and it hadn't ended well.

In a strange way, his go-slow approach was making her want him all the more. Her body felt alive and tingling with anticipation, reacting to every look he cast her way, every touch of his hand or brush of his lips. She picked up her champagne glass and took another sip, listening to the sounds of the birds settling in the shrubbery, the throaty croak of a frog on the bank of the pond and then the resounding *plop* as it went below the silvery surface. She rose from the garden chair and wandered over to the nearest flowerbed, bent her head to smell the heady clove-like scent of night stocks.

She glanced towards the house and caught a glimpse of Louis in the kitchen, preparing their food. As if he sensed her gaze on him, he looked up from what he was doing and locked gazes with her. A hot rush of longing travelled through her body and she began walking towards the house as if drawn by a powerful magnet. She *did* have the courage to go to him. His touch had awakened it in her. The needs raging in her body refused to be put on hold. It was as if a fever had gripped her—a fever of longing to feel Louis' mouth on hers, his arms holding her close to his body.

When she got to the kitchen, Louis wiped his hands on a tea towel and smiled. 'Too cold out there now?'

Ivy stepped up to him and looked up into his grey-blue eyes. 'I kind of like the heat in here more.'

His pupils flared and his gaze dipped to her mouth, his hands settling on her hips. 'You're not making this easy for me, Ivy. I'm supposed to be giving you dinner before we do anything else.'

She moved closer, winding her arms around his neck, her breasts pushing against his chest. Any shyness she might have felt was gone, obliterated by the overwhelming need powering through her body. The need he had brought to life in her flesh. 'I'm not hungry for food. I'm hungry for you.'

He groaned and covered her mouth with his in a long, drugging kiss that made her senses go into a tailspin. His tongue mated with hers and her spine loosened and her knees wobbled. One of his hands cupped her breast, his touch light and yet sending thousands of shivers through her sensitive flesh. He pulled her dress down a fraction and began to caress her breast with his lips and tongue, teasing her nipple into a tight peak, tantalising her with the sensation of his stubble against her soft skin.

Ivy whimpered with longing for more of his touch, the passionate need in the core of her body pulsating, pounding. He moved to her other breast, exposing it to his hungry, smouldering gaze and placing his mouth on the upper curve, then trailing his tongue over and around her nipple, taking it into his mouth and gently sucking on it. The nerves in her tender flesh rioted with ecstasy, triggering even more flutters and flickers and flames in her lower body.

Louis lifted his head to look at her with eyes dark and glittering with lust. 'Dinner can wait. I want you.' His voice was low and deep and gravelly, sending a shiver whispering down her spine.

'I want you too, so, so much,' Ivy said. 'I've never experienced anything like this before. It's like my body hasn't been alive until now.'

He framed her face in his hands, his expression serious. 'I won't do anything you're not comfortable doing.'

Ivy stroked his stubbled jaw and gazed into his

eyes. 'I know you won't. That's why you're the only person I could ask to help me. I trust you.'

A fleeting shadow went through his gaze before it lowered to her mouth once more. He drew in a ragged breath and took one of her hands, his fingers warm and strong around hers. His eyes met hers and he smiled a slow smile that made her heart slip sideways. 'Let's go upstairs.'

Ivy went with him up the grand staircase and he led her to his master suite at the other end of the wide corridor from her bedroom. Her skin was tight all over, her heart rate picking up, her senses on high alert. She was attuned to his every movement, not out of fear but out of excitement. The twilight was still filtering into the room, giving it a muted and intimate glow, and when Louis didn't reach for the light switch she wondered if he'd remembered her confession about not being comfortable undressing unless the lights were out. It touched her that he was being so patient and understanding with her.

He stood with her next to the king-sized bed, his hands loosely holding hers. His gaze roved over her face, lingering on her mouth and then coming back to her eyes. 'Remember, you're the one in control here. I want this to be perfect for you.'

'Everything's been perfect so far.' Ivy slipped her hands out of his and began to unbutton his shirt. 'I want to feel your skin on mine.' Her heart was fluttering, but with excitement rather than nerves.

It was empowering to know he would be patient with her, not rushing or pushing her to do things she wasn't ready to do. Somehow it made her feel more emboldened than she had ever felt before, the needs of her body overtaking the paralysing fears in her mind. Funny how those fears were retreating further and further into the background, every magical touch of his melting them away.

Louis shrugged himself out of his shirt and then reached to undo the clip holding her hair on top of her head. It cascaded down around her shoulders. He swept her hair to one side and lowered his mouth to the soft skin just below her ear, and she shivered as his lips and tongue subjected her to feather-light caresses.

'You smell beautiful—like flowers and summer—and I can't wait to taste you all over.' His tone had a roughened edge, as if he was fighting to keep his control in check.

Her own control was facing a similar battle. The shy part of her nature wanted to put the brakes on before he could act on his erotic promise but the sensually awakened part of her relished the thought of him caressing her in such an intimate way. 'I want to taste you too.'

She brought her mouth to his neck in the shallow dish between his clavicles and pressed her lips to the saltiness of his skin. He shuddered under her touch and brought her closer to the jutting hardness of his body. Ivy grew emboldened by the impact she was having on him and kissed his neck again, this time using her tongue in kitten-like licks.

He made a sound at the back of his throat and, with one hand pressed to the small of her back, brought the other to cup her breast. 'I want to see you. All of you. Do you want me to undress you or would you feel more comfortable doing it yourself?'

Ivy was touched that he'd asked rather than assumed he could go ahead. 'I want you to do it.' She could hardly believe she was saying it, but it was true. She felt totally comfortable with him peeling the clothes from her body. Besides, the room was even darker now, so she didn't feel as exposed as she might have done.

Louis slowly slid her dress down her body, his eyes glinting in the low light as her breasts were finally uncovered. Ivy resisted the urge to cover herself and watched as his gaze lingered on her curves. Her dress went to a puddle at her feet and she stepped out of it, standing in nothing but a tiny pair of knickers.

'You are every bit as beautiful as I imagined…' His voice had a raw, earthy quality to it that made her desire for him go up another notch. His hands cradled both her breasts and he bent his head to caress them with his lips and tongue. Ivy shivered as she watched his dark head lower to her naked flesh, the sheer eroticism of his action making her inner core contract with want. He knelt down in front of her and kissed his way down her body—below her breasts, over her ribcage, her abdomen, and then to the top of her lacy underwear. Ivy stiffened, suddenly shy at revealing the most intimate part of her body.

Louis steadied her with his hands on her hips, his eyes meeting hers. 'Don't be shy, *ma chérie*.'

She bit her lip and stepped out of his hold, covering her breasts with her hands. 'I'm sorry. I don't think I can go any further.' Her feverish body screamed, *No! Don't stop now!* But she couldn't overcome the fear he might find her repulsive.

He straightened and came over to her, resting his hands on the top of her shoulders. 'Look at me, Ivy.'

Ivy slowly brought her gaze up to his, her cheeks so hot they felt like they were going to explode. 'See? I told you. I'm an uptight prude.'

He gave her shoulders a gentle squeeze. 'Tell me what's worrying you. Did that jerk say something to you about this part of you too?'

She looked at his chin rather than meet his gaze. 'No, but I'm… I'm worried you won't like the way I look down there. You sleep with so many women. What if I'm a freak compared to them?'

He placed a finger beneath her chin and brought her gaze back to his. 'Women's bodies come in all shapes and sizes. You're perfect just the way you are. You don't need to be ashamed of any part of your body.'

'I know, but I am, and I can't seem to help it.'

Louis stroked his finger over her bottom lip, his eyes shining. 'I love everything I've seen so far.'

'Really?' Ivy lowered her hands from covering her breasts, aching to feel them pressed up against the naked skin of his muscular chest.

'Really.' He devoured her breasts with his gaze and a hot spurt of longing shot to her core.

She moved closer so her breasts were against his chest, her arms going back around his neck. 'Thanks for keeping the lights off.' In semi-darkness she could hide her secret thoughts and feelings…she could feel less exposed, less vulnerable. She was ready to give herself to him physically but she wanted her emotions kept in the shadows where they couldn't be seen.

'That's fine. I can make love to you by Braille.'

Ivy laughed, shivering at the thought of his hands and lips and tongue reading every inch of her flesh. 'You mean you haven't given up on me yet?'

His eyes held hers in a heart-stopping lock. 'Do you want me to give up?'

'No,' she said, standing on tiptoes to press a kiss to his mouth. 'I want you to make love to me. That's why we came here tonight. I need to do this.'

'Then let's do this,' Louis said and brought his mouth down to hers.

Ivy sighed with pure pleasure as his mouth subjected hers to a passionate exploration. His tongue playfully teased hers into a sexy tango, one of his hands coming up to cradle her face, the other to hold the back of her head, his fingers splaying through her hair. Desire flared and flamed in her lower body, longing coursing through her flesh like lashing tongues of flame. She was pressed so close to him she could feel every hard ridge and contour of his body, the heat and potency of his arousal against her stirring her female flesh into a frenzy of want. She could feel the secret preparation of her body, the dewy wetness of female arousal and the low, deep pulse in her core.

Louis raised his mouth off hers and led her to the bed. He whipped off the covers, then his shirt and trousers, and drew her down beside him on the bed. He was still wearing his underwear, but she couldn't take her eyes off his aroused length tenting the fabric, but was too shy to reach for him. What if she did something wrong? What if he didn't like her touch?

'You can touch me if you want.' His voice was deep and rough with desire.

'What if I don't do it right?'

He took her hand and placed it on his erection over his underwear, a ripple of pleasure passing over his face at her touch. Then he peeled his underwear out of the way and placed her hand on him, skin on skin. 'You won't hurt me. That's it, hold me in your hand.'

He was so thick and strong, like velvet-covered steel, and her intimate muscles quivered at the thought of him entering her. She stroked him harder, enjoying the guttural sounds he was making, enjoying the power it gave her to tantalise him with her touch.

'My turn now.' He removed her hand from his body and gently pushed her back down on the mattress, propping himself up on one elbow, the other hand stroking her from her breasts to her belly and back again in long, slow strokes until her back was almost arching off the bed. He went lower with his hand, cupping her mound over her knickers. She moaned against his hand, wanting more but unsure how to ask for it. He left his hand where it was and kissed her mouth again, long, slow and deep. It gave her time to get used to feeling him touching her, holding the most sensitive part of her body without pushing her to go any further. But she wanted to go further, she wanted to go all the way. Her body was hungry and aching for his possession.

'I want you.' Her voice came out breathless.

'Patience, *ma petite*.' His tone had a sexy, raspy edge that made her shiver all the more with longing. 'There's no rush.'

Ivy took his hand and placed it on her female flesh. 'I want you to touch me. I need you to.'

His eyes darkened until there was only a narrow rim of grey-blue visible around the bottomless black of his pupils. 'How about we take these off, hmm?' He peeled away her knickers and she lifted her hips to help him, way beyond shyness with her body raging with such unstoppable lust. He stroked the seam of her body, slowly, torturously slowly, and every nerve in her pelvis fizzed like a firework. Hot streaks of sensation ran down her legs, a warm pool forming at the base of her spine and spreading to her core. He brought his mouth down to her and stroked his tongue where his finger had just been. It was shockingly intimate and yet she didn't flinch or shy away from it. She was too far gone for that. She whimpered, gasped and throbbed with longing.

He lifted his mouth off her and separated her folds with his fingers, his gaze devouring her female form as if it was the most beautiful thing he'd ever seen. 'You're gorgeous…' His voice was husky, his touch exquisitely gentle.

Ivy sucked in a much-needed breath and instinctively spread her legs wider, her heart racing with excitement. 'Are you going to do what I think you're going to do?' Her voice was so breathless it came out like a strangled whisper.

'Only if you want me to.'

She swallowed. 'I want you to.' Never had she wanted anything more. Her body was on fire and flickering with delicious sensations.

Louis brought his mouth to her again, his lips and tongue playing with her female flesh, finally triggering a powerful rush that seemingly came from nowhere and everywhere at once. Waves and ripples of pleasure washed through her pelvis, making her writhe and cry out as if she was possessed by a paranormal entity.

Ivy gasped and flung her head back against the bed, her chest heaving, her body limp as the aftershocks gradually faded. 'Oh, God, that was… I don't know how to describe it.'

Louis came up on one elbow and smiled down at her. 'It will get better.'

She had no idea how it ever could. She had never experienced anything so earth-shattering. She tiptoed her fingers down his sternum all the way to his rock-hard abdomen. 'Aren't you going to…?'

He captured her hand before it could go any lower and pressed a kiss to the middle of her palm. 'Not right now.' His expression became unreadable and she could sense him pulling away as if an invisible drawbridge had come up between them.

She blinked at him in surprise. 'But aren't you…?'

He pressed a finger to her lips to halt her speech. 'This is about your pleasure, not mine.'

Ivy brushed his hand away and grasped him by the shoulder. 'But isn't making love meant to be a two-way thing?'

'Yes, but there's plenty of time. We've got all night.' He rolled away and picked up his shirt and trousers from the floor and proceeded to put them back on.

Ivy pulled the bed sheet up over her nakedness, wondering why he'd called a halt when it was so obvious he desired her. *We've got all night.* But wouldn't most guys want to make the most of it?

She was starting to wonder if one night was going to be enough for her. He had awakened needs and desires in her that thrilled and delighted her. But what was going to happen when this night was over? Back to being friends only. 'Is this about your one-night-only rule? You can't bring yourself to sleep with me more than once? Why do you even have such a dumb rule?'

Louis' jaw tightened. 'I've always been a fan of the casual one-nighter—hence my moniker, Mr Amazing One-Night Stand. Brief hook-ups are less complicated, given my work commitments. I don't like being tied down in a relationship when I have other demands on my time. But a few months ago I allowed a hook-up to stretch out to three weeks. Big mistake. The woman became increasingly attached and started dropping hints about moving in with me. I broke things off as gently as I could but it didn't go well.'

He speared a hand through his hair and blew out a breath before continuing, 'She was clearly heart-broken and I felt awful about causing her that much pain, especially as we'd both agreed at the beginning it was only a short-term fling. She stalked me for weeks on end. I had to block her on my phone and email, to stop the bombardment of calls and texts and emails. It was embarrassing when she'd show up at work in tears, desperate to talk to me. Once she turned up in another city where I was presenting at a conference. Since then, I made a promise to myself never to date anyone longer than twenty-four hours.'

Ivy got off the bed, bringing the sheet with her as a sarong around her body. 'So, you're letting one woman who didn't know how to deal with rejection ruin your chance to ever be in a proper, fulfilling relationship?'

'But I've never wanted anything more than casual relationships.' His tone was curt. 'I've seen the way fulfilling relationships change over time into full-on war.'

She frowned. 'Your parents?'

His lip curled. 'My parents and yours and numerous others.'

Ivy could hardly argue with that. Her parents had seemed happy enough until her father's affair had been uncovered. The affair had been going on for close to a year. No wonder her mother had gone off the rails once she'd found out. 'I know not everyone ends up happy forever, but at least it's worth a try. Falling in love with someone and building a life together is all I've ever wanted.'

'Good luck with that.' Cynicism laced his tone.

Ivy chewed her lip for a moment. 'So, why did you date that woman for as long as you did?'

Louis blew out a breath, his brow creased in a frown. 'She was good company, easy to get along with and—'

'Good in bed?'

He gave her an unreadable look. 'It's not a habit of mine to discuss previous lovers with other people.'

'That's very reassuring.'

His eyes held hers for a beat or two. 'What happens between us stays between us. You have my word on that.'

Ivy went up to him and placed a hand on his forearm. 'Thank you. I sometimes lie awake at night worrying what those guys I dated are saying about me to their friends. It's one of the reasons I haven't gone on any other dates.'

He placed his hand over hers, his fingers warm and strong. His grey-blue eyes drifted to her mouth and back again. 'You don't kiss like a Victorian prude.' His other arm came around her body, drawing her closer to his deliciously hard frame. Every female cell in her body rejoiced at the contact, her breasts tingled, her lower body contracted and her heart began to pick up its pace.

Ivy reached up and stroked her hand over the

prickly stubble of his lean jaw. 'How many Victorian prudes have you kissed?'

His eyes became sexily hooded, his hand going to the small of her back, bringing her even closer. 'I don't kiss and tell, remember?'

'Good to know.' Her voice dropped to a whisper, desire beating with an insistent pulse between her legs. She breathed in the male scent of him, the salty hint of perspiration and the sharp citrus notes of his aftershave. 'Louis…about the Victorian prude thing…'

She glanced up at him again. 'Remember when my parents got divorced in my early teens? Well, Ronan probably told you how crazy our mother went, although he didn't see a lot of it, as he was at boarding school and then university. She had so many boyfriends coming and going. It was like she was trying to outdo my father, to punish him for having that affair for so long. She wasn't choosy in who she brought home either. It was terrifying at times to suddenly confront a strange man on his way to the bathroom or in the kitchen, helping himself to stuff.'

Louis frowned. 'Did anyone touch you or…?'

She shook her head. 'No, thankfully not, but I felt creeped out by it all. And then, I'd visit Dad at his flat, where he was living with his new girlfriend. He would act all lovey-dovey, the way he used to act with Mum. I felt so angry, but I couldn't say anything, as I didn't want to lose him out of my life. But I did in the end, anyway.'

'It must have been a terribly confusing time for you,' Louis said, still frowning.

'It was… I feel a bit silly about it now. I mean, I'm almost thirty and I've let something that happened so long ago stop me from living the life I want to live. But I truly couldn't bear the thought of having sex with someone I didn't know and trust like my mother did after Dad left.'

His look was long and thoughtful, as if her words resonated with his own situation. 'You coped the best way you could. Don't be so hard on yourself.'

She gave him a crooked smile. 'But all that's going to change now you've helped me embrace my sensuality. I don't know how to thank you.'

He brought his mouth to the right side of her forehead, his lips moving against her skin in teasing little brushes that made the hairs on her head stand up and a warm, treacly sensation flow down her spine. He moved his lips down her face—the sensitive spots in front of and below her ear—and she shuddered with the tickling pleasure of his touch. He kissed the edges of her mouth without actually touching her lips, ramping up her desire for his kiss to a frenzied, fiery ache in her flesh.

Ivy gripped him by the shoulders, her body so close to his she could feel every hard ridge and solid plane, sending a wave of intense longing through her. 'Kiss me, Louis. Don't make me beg.'

He framed her face in his hands, his eyes as dark as outer space. 'If I kiss you, I might not want to stop.'

She licked her lips and held his gaze. 'Why would that be a problem if I don't want you to stop?'

He leaned his forehead on hers, their breaths mingling intimately in the space between their faces. 'I thought I had the willpower, the self-control, to talk you out of your crazy plan to lose your virginity to me.' He eased back to look down at her. 'But it seems I overestimated the limits of my control.'

Ivy traced the outline of his mouth with her finger, her heart beating a tattoo in her chest. 'I want you to make love to me. I want you to be my first lover. It feels right for it to be you and not someone I don't care a fig about. Or someone who might talk about me to their friends.'

He brushed her hair back from her forehead, his eyes dark and serious. 'It's only for tonight. After that, we go our separate ways. I can't offer anything else.'

'I don't want anything else.' Ivy wrapped her arms around his neck and stood on tiptoe as his head came down. His mouth covered hers in a fireball kiss, sending sparks shooting through her body. She opened to him and his tongue teased hers into a dance that mimicked the most erotic of connections two humans could have with each other. Desire leapt and burned and blazed in her flesh as he increased the pressure of his lips on hers. She pushed herself against him, hungry for his touch, aching for his possession.

His hands skated down the sides of her body, peeling the bed sheet away like a skin and covering one of her breasts with the broad expanse of his hand. His touch was gentle and yet electric, sending hot sparks through her flesh. Her nipple went to a tight bud, the soft flesh of her breast tingling. He removed his hand and replaced it with his mouth, exploring her in intimate detail. He rolled his tongue over and around her nipple, then took it into his mouth, gently sucking on it, releasing a shower of pleasurable sensations through her body. He moved to her other breast, subjecting it to the same passionate exploration until she was gasping and writhing with the need to feel more.

Louis brought his mouth back to hers in another drugging kiss, his arms going back around her body, one of his hands cupping the naked curve of her bottom. He groaned against her lips, his kiss deepening, his breathing as hectic as hers. 'God, I want you so badly. How did I ever think this wasn't going to happen eventually?'

Ivy stroked his jaw and leaned into the throbbing pulse of his lower body. 'I want you too.'

He held her from him and locked gazes. 'By the way, are you using any contraception?'

'I'm on a low-dose pill.' She twisted her mouth in a rueful manner. 'Not that I've needed it until now. It was just wishful thinking on my part.'

'I always use condoms in any case but it's good to be doubly sure there won't be an unwanted pregnancy. That's a complication both of us could do without.'

'Okay. Sounds good.' Ivy had wanted children since she'd been a child herself. The thought of never having a family of her own was her worst nightmare. But she could hardly tell Louis that. He was so adamant about not settling down and she was not going to compromise on something so important to her. Besides, she was not involved with him with the goal of happy-ever-after. Louis wasn't the answer to her fairy-tale fantasy—he was just the answer to her V problem. She was engaging his services to help her get in the dating game with more confidence. Why would she be interested in a future with a renowned playboy? That wasn't a future—that was a recipe for heartbreak. And she wanted no part of it.

Louis sourced a condom from his wallet in the pocket of his trousers and then, stepping out of his clothes, led her back to the bed. The moon had risen and cast the room in a silvery glow. Strangely, her shyness about being naked in front of him wasn't an issue. All she could think about was finding release from the tender ache between her legs. An ache he had triggered with his magical touch. Ivy drank in the sight of his fully aroused body, all the strong planes and contours of male flesh in its prime. Her desire for him rose again like an unquenchable thirst. 'How many condoms did you bring?'

'Enough.' His eyes glinted and he tore the packet open and applied the condom.

Ivy stroked him with her hand, enjoying the sensation of his powerful flesh quivering from her touch. 'I never thought I'd feel comfortable doing this but with you it feels so...so right.'

He pressed her back down on the bed, his expression clouding. 'It feels better than it probably should, given our situation.'

Ivy frowned. 'What do you mean?'

His eyes went back and forth between each of hers and then drifted to her mouth. He drew in a deep breath and gave a half-smile that looked a little forced. He brushed her hair back from her face, his eyes dark and unreadable. 'Is one night going to be enough for you?'

Ivy licked her suddenly dry lips and aimed her gaze at his chin. 'That's what we agreed, right? Those are your rules and I'm fine with that.' Was she, though? A niggling doubt wormed its way into her mind. The exquisite pleasure he'd made her feel so far had made her hungry, ravenous, greedy for more. How was one measly little night going to satisfy her?

He lifted her chin with his finger and meshed his gaze with hers. 'Yeah, that's what we agreed. One night and one night only.'

Ivy pulled his head back down to hers. 'Then we'd better get on with it.'

He covered her mouth in a kiss that spoke of desperate passion only just held in check. His tongue flickered against hers, erotically mimicking the full possession of her body she craved so much. Ivy moved against him, silently urging him to assuage the throbbing ache of desire in her flesh. One of his legs hitched over hers, the sexy tangle of their limbs arousing in itself.

'I want you so much.' He groaned the words against her mouth, his body hot and hard against her.

'Me too.' Ivy could barely speak for the rapacious hunger vibrating in her body.

Louis brought himself to her entrance, nudging her with his tip but not going any further. 'If you don't feel comfortable at any point, let me know.'

'Okay.'

His first thrust was shallow and gentle, but Ivy was too impatient to wait and lifted her hips to receive him, her hands going to his taut buttocks to urge him on. He gave an agonised groan and went a little deeper, the slickness of her body welcoming him. He stilled his movements, his breathing hectic. 'Are you okay?'

'Don't stop. Please keep going.' Her body was on fire, flickers and, flames and fizzing sensations travelling throughout her pelvis and down the backs of her legs.

Louis continued to thrust, but she sensed he was holding himself back out of consideration for her. But her body was enjoying every inch of his powerful length and was crying out for more. She gripped him harder by the buttocks and lifted her hips to meet each downward thrust. He sucked in a harsh breath and his rhythm increased, the thrusts becoming deeper and faster, sending her senses reeling. Her body wrapped tight around him, his intimate invasion not quite enough to send her over the edge into the abyss. But then he began to caress her with his fingers, giving her the extra friction she needed to soar. She threw her head back and gasped out sobbing cries of release, her body shaking, quivering, thrashing with the sheer force rocketing through her.

Ivy was still suffering the aftershocks when Louis found his own release and she held him through it, enjoying the way his body tensed and then finally broke free from the restraints he'd put on it. There was something so deeply primal about his groans and almost savage about his orgasm. It thrilled her that she had brought him so undone by her touch, her body, her caresses.

Louis rolled away, disposed of the condom and then lay back and flung an arm across his eyes, his chest still heaving. 'Dear God in heaven...'

Ivy propped herself up on one elbow by his side, her hand stroking down his chest. 'Was it good for you?' She couldn't quite remove the note of uncertainty in her voice.

He turned his head her way and smiled a lopsided smile, and something in her chest turned over. He covered her hand with his, anchoring on the thud-thud-thud of his heart. 'Better than good—amazing.'

She leaned forward and pressed a soft kiss to his lips. 'Thanks for making it so special for me.'

He tucked a wayward strand of hair back behind her ear, his gaze locked on hers. 'I didn't hurt you?'

She smiled and tiptoed her fingers across his toned pectoral muscles. 'Not a bit. I read somewhere that the only way you can tell if a woman is a virgin is if she tells you and you believe her. All that stuff about broken and bleeding hymens is a bit of a myth. Most women and girls damage their hymen doing sports during childhood or using tampons when they get their periods.'

'True, but sex can still be uncomfortable for a woman if her partner isn't considerate.'

Ivy lifted her hand to his head and toyed with his short-cropped hair. 'But you were very considerate.'

His expression was warm with tenderness, his hand going to her hip and rolling her towards him. 'If I was truly considerate, I'd take you downstairs and feed you the delicious dinner my housekeeper prepared.'

'I'm sensing a "but" at the end of that sentence.'

He grinned and swiftly turned her over so her back was against the mattress, his body half-covering hers. 'But I want to do this first.' And his mouth came down to hers.

Louis kissed her slowly and leisurely at first, but then a storm of need began to barrel through him, and he deepened the kiss with a commanding thrust of his tongue. She opened to him like a flower and he groaned at the back of his throat and explored her sweet mouth as if it was the last kiss he would ever have. Her lips were soft and yielding, passionate and responsive, and his blood pounded with renewed desire. Making love to her had shocked him to the core. Not in a bad way, but in a way he hadn't been expecting. Normally sex was just sex, a physical thing he enjoyed like any other man. But with Ivy something felt different. Not just because it was her first time, although he had to admit that had made it rather special—memorably special. But the taste of her skin, the response of her body, stirred him in a way no other lover had done before.

Louis rained kisses down her body, lingering over her breasts before going to the silk of her inner thighs. He teased her with his lips and tongue, working his way to the feminine heart of her body. She gasped as he anointed her with his tongue, her body shuddering through an orgasm, his own body desperate for intimate connection with the tight slickness of hers.

Ivy reached for him and he only just had time to put on another condom in his haste to bury himself in her honeyed core. The tumult built to a crescendo inside him, her movements so in tune with his, sending his senses reeling. The heat, the musk of mating, the glide of aroused male flesh against velvet female flesh, sent him into the stratosphere where no thought could reside, only pleasure…mind-blowing, skin-tingling bliss…

In the quiet, restful moments afterwards, a stray thought managed to get through the firewall of Louis' mind.

One night, huh? Are you sure that's going to be enough?

He tried to think of something else but, with Ivy's soft hand gently stroking the flank of his thigh, he knew the hunger he had for her was not going to be satisfied by one night. But he would have to accept that and stick with the plan. Continuing this any-

longer than a night was tempting but too dangerous. It was a physical hunger, nothing else, and it
would fade as long as he didn't fuel it. He didn't *do*
anything else. Couldn't do anything else. *Wouldn't*
do anything else.

But, oh, how he wanted to.

CHAPTER SIX

IVY WOKE TO find herself alone in bed early the next morning. Louis had told her he was a restless sleeper who often got up during the night to work but she hadn't seen him bring a laptop with him—although she had noticed a well-appointed study downstairs. Perhaps he had put in a few hours on his latest project or gone for a run or something.

She pushed aside the sense of disappointment that Louis hadn't woken up beside her and instead focussed on the positives. She was no longer a virgin. Her mission was accomplished with two weeks to spare until she turned thirty. Her body felt different, somehow, more alive and sensitive than ever before. Even the sensation of the sheets against her skin was heightened. It was as if her nerves had shifted position.

She pushed the bedcovers off and slipped on the satin bathrobe she'd brought with her. The smooth fabric on her body felt as delicious as a caress and she couldn't wait to feel Louis' touch again. She squeezed her thighs together. Her inner muscles gave the faintest of protests and a frisson passed over her flesh. How wonderful would it be to spend the rest of the weekend together, making love again—and not just this weekend, but the one after and the one after and...

Ivy was pulled away from her thoughts as if by the sudden tug of a marionette's strings. *One night and one night only.* That was what she'd agreed on and it was all Louis was offering. She knew enough about him to know he could be stubborn when his mind was made up.

Wouldn't it be better if she avoided the 'morning after the night before' scene she was dreading? How could she look at him now and see him as only a friend and not the most amazing lover a woman could ask for? Her body was already craving him. How would she hide her longing from him? It was better to leave before he came back from wherever he'd gone during the night. Before he saw how much she wanted him to continue their fling. Before her feelings got involved any more than they already were. Before she made a complete and utter fool of herself by begging him to extend their fling beyond the one night they'd agreed on.

She reached for her phone and organised a taxi back to London.

Hopefully she would be halfway home before he even knew she had gone.

Louis hadn't slept so soundly for years—even if it had only been until just before dawn. Maybe it was the Cotswolds air. Maybe it was breaking his sex drought. *Maybe it was Ivy...*

He'd left her sleeping in the early hours, not trusting himself to wake up beside her without wanting to make love to her again. Or tweaking the rules so they spent the rest of the weekend down here. But he had no business tweaking the rules. He had done as she requested and there was no need to take things any further.

Weird, but he had no regrets about last night. How could he when it was the best sex he'd ever had? Sensual, meaningful, memorable, tender…and yet racy. His body tingled at the thought of Ivy's touch. His lips remembered the taste and texture of hers. Every cell in his body wanted her with a grinding hunger.

But their night together was over.

It was Saturday morning and their relationship had to go back to normal. Normal? How normal was it that every time he looked at her now he would recall the softness of her mouth under his, the stroke of her hands, the warm, velvet grip of her body? He shuddered and groaned as desire swept through him like a tide, heating and hardening his flesh to the point of pain.

He went for a long run along the country lanes, trying to summon his self-control. Maybe he should tweak the rules. Maybe she needed more than one night to gain even more confidence. She'd told him how her parents' break-up had contributed to her uneasiness with intimacy, and it had made him realise even more how stressful and difficult her adolescence had been. Hadn't he carried his own hangups from his childhood?

You're rationalising—you just want to continue your fling with her.

Louis knew the danger of extending their fling. It was one of the reasons he'd been reluctant to start it in the first place. Ivy wasn't like the other women he dated—not because they hadn't been nice women, with lots to offer. But he could always switch off his feelings when he had casual dates. He was a master at it. But with Ivy those unwanted feelings had a habit of slipping under his guard, making him hunger for things he had so long suppressed or told himself he didn't really want.

And then there was the other complication of his friendship with her brother. Ronan would never forgive him for hurting Ivy. And how could he avoid hurting her if he continued to sleep with her without offering her the whole package she yearned for— marriage, babies and forever love? A package he had no intention of offering to anyone. Ever.

Louis came back from his run and showered and

dressed before going to Ivy's room. The door of her room was closed, so he gave it a gentle tap.

'Ivy? Are you up? Time for breakfast before we head back to London.'

There was no answer, so he opened the door and went in. The bed had been stripped and the duvet neatly folded back to wait for fresh sheets to be placed on later. It took him a moment to register what he was seeing—or not seeing. There was no trace of Ivy in the room. Her luggage was gone and when he checked the *en suite* no trace of her toiletries remained. All that was left was the faint trace of her perfume lingering in the air.

There was something strangely mocking about that bare and empty bed. He was the one who normally left before his casual dates woke on the rare occasions he spent the whole night with anyone. He assiduously avoided the morning-after scenes where a date would drop hints about wanting to see him again. Why had Ivy left? *How* had she left?

And then he saw the note propped next to the bedside lamp. He walked across the room and snatched it up, unfolding the rectangle of paper to read:

Thanks for last night. I didn't want to wake you, so caught a cab back home. I have to get ready for Paris next week.
Your friend, Ivy

He stared at the word 'friend' for so long, he became cross-eyed. He sucked in a harsh breath, scrunched the note into a ball and tossed it on the bed. The bed where he had made love to her last night. Not simply had hook-up sex, but actually made love. Her first time had been *his* first time feeling more than needing an itch to be scratched. His first time feeling more than lust, feeling something far more complicated.

Why had she left without seeing him face to face? Was she feeling uncomfortable? Embarrassed? Regretful? He took out his phone and called her number, but it went through to voice mail.

'Call me.' He spoke more curtly than he'd intended, annoyed with himself for not anticipating her leaving. He was rarely blindsided by people these days. He never got close enough to anyone for them to surprise him. It didn't sit well with him to be the one left behind, staring at the empty bed where he'd had the best sex of his life.

One night not enough for you, huh? His conscience jeered from the sidelines.

Louis ground his teeth so hard, he thought he'd be taking his meals through a straw for the next month.

No, one night wasn't enough—so he was going to do something about it.

Ivy was tidying up the back office of the antiques store for her elderly boss, Mr Thornley, when she heard a customer come into the shop. She glanced at the CCTV monitor on the desk and her heart missed a beat—and then raced, as if it needed an emergency dose of beta blockers. Louis had only once before come in to the shop and her heart hadn't threatened to go into overdrive then. But that had been before she had slept with him, experienced for one night the phenomenal magic of being in his arms.

She wiped her suddenly damp palms on the front of her skirt and went out to greet him, painting a smile on her face. 'Hiya, Louis.'

She was proud of how normal she sounded. Who said she couldn't switch back to being friends with him without a stumble? Even if every cell of her body was acutely aware of him and longed to feel his arms go around her to hold her close.

His grey-blue eyes ran over her skirt and blouse and she wondered if he was recalling every inch of her naked flesh and how it had felt against his own. His mouth was set in a firm line and there was a muscle twitching in his jaw. 'Why did you leave without saying goodbye on Saturday, or calling me as I asked?' His tone was as curt as the short message he had left on her voice mail the other day. A message she had chosen not to obey.

Ivy raised her chin, sending him a tiny flash of her gaze. 'You didn't ask—you demanded.'

His eyes warred with hers for a long moment. Then his tense features softened a fraction and his voice lowered to a rich, deep burr. 'I was worried about you. I thought you might be feeling some regret about our night together.'

Ivy schooled her features into 'Ms Modern Hook-Up' mode. 'Why should I be feeling regret? We spent the night together as agreed. It went well and I went home. End of.'

A frown pulled at his brow and his mouth flattened once more. 'But why not wait until I drove you back?'

She turned to straighten some papers on the cluttered desk. 'I thought it was better to go before you talked me into staying the whole weekend with you.'

There was a silence so intense, the soft ticking of the French carriage clock on the desk sounded like hammer blows.

Louis gave an incredulous laugh. 'You thought I was going to ask you for an extension?'

Ivy turned back to face him, her look pointed. 'Weren't you?'

A shutter came down at the back of his gaze, screening his thoughts, hiding his feelings, locking her out. 'I only do one-night stands, remember?'

Ivy folded her arms across her body and lifted her right hand to her mouth, tapping against her lips as if studying a particularly interesting artefact. 'Then why are you here now? It's too late for lunch or even coffee. Besides, I'm flying to Paris early tomorrow, so—'

'So am I.'

Ivy stared at him. 'You are?' She disguised a tight swallow. 'Are you seeing a client or…?' She couldn't complete the rest of her sentence. She didn't want to know if he planned to hook up with someone while he was in France. He often travelled for work, and was rarely in London for more than a week at a time. He would no doubt go back to his playboy lifestyle now and she would have to suffer seeing him in the gossip pages with a host of other women who were happy with the brief encounters he offered them.

'I have a couple of projects going on in Paris that I need to check,' he said. 'Where are you staying?'

'I haven't had time to book my accommodation yet,' Ivy said, unfolding her arms. 'My boss normally organises it when I go away on a business trip for him, but his wife had a fall on Sunday night, so he's been a bit distracted. I was going to find a room tonight.'

'Stay with me at my apartment.' His expression was still difficult to read but something about the incredible stillness of his posture made her suspect he was holding his breath.

She ran the tip of her tongue over her lips, not sure what to make of his invitation. Wanting to accept it but not sure if it was wise to do so. Stay with him in Paris. The most romantic city in the world. The city of love. 'Why do you want me to stay with you?'

His eyes darkened and he crossed the distance to where she was standing in two or three strides. He took one of her hands in his and stroked his thumb over her racing pulse. 'You know why.' His voice was so deep it could have come from the centre of the earth.

Ivy decided to play it cool. 'Do I? Last time we spoke you made it clear we were a one-night thing. Are we going to be friends or lovers in Paris?'

His thumb stroked over the fleshy part of her thumb, triggering a storm of sensations that travelled from her hand to her core in a fizzing fire trail. His eyes held hers in an unwavering lock, making her spine tingle, as though sherbet were slowly trickling through her vertebrae. 'We can be both.'

'But I thought—'

'How long will you be in Paris?'

'Wednesday till Friday.'

'Can you stay until Sunday?' he asked.

'I guess so… But I thought you said—'

'Five days in Paris. That's all I'm offering. Take it or leave it.' His tone was so businesslike and clinical, yet his hand holding hers seemed to communicate a more desperate plea. A plea that her own body was communicating with a raised pulse and a skipping heartbeat and bated breath.

Ivy chewed one side of her lip and looked down

at their joined hands. She recalled his hands on her most intimate flesh and something turned over in her stomach. One night was never going to be enough but would another five cure this sweet, torturous ache he alone triggered in her body? Probably not, but she would at least have more memories to keep when the time was over. She slowly brought her gaze back up to his. 'I'll come with you to Paris.'

His smile was lazy, but it ignited a flare in his eyes that made her heart skip another beat. 'Good.' He brought her hand up to his lips and kissed her bent knuckles, still holding her gaze. 'I'll see you in the morning.' He released her hand, his expression turning rueful. 'I would have suggested dinner tonight but it's my mother's birthday. I wouldn't want to give her the wrong impression about us.'

Ivy would have liked to meet his parents in an effort to understand him better, but she was reluctant to voice it out loud. They were having a fling, not a relationship that followed a more traditional pattern of dating, courtship, marriage. She had no right to be offended that he didn't offer to introduce her to his family. She wasn't a permanent fixture in his life or at least not in a romantic sense. She had never envisaged him as a romantic partner, never allowed herself to think of him in any way other than as her brother's friend. But one kiss had changed something inside her, which was faintly worrying. She was meant to have kept her emotions out of

their arrangement. The last thing she needed was
to complicate her life by falling in love with a man
who had locked his heart away.

'I totally understand. Just imagine if I brought
you home with me to see my mum. She'd book a
wedding planner on the spot and she'd probably beg
to be my bridesmaid.'

Louis' smile didn't quite reach his eyes. 'Then
it's best we keep this trip to Paris to ourselves.'

'Fine. Good plan.'

He moved closer again and leaned down to press
a soft kiss to her lips. When he pulled back, her lips
clung to his like silk snagging on something rough.
His mouth came down again, firmer, warmer, more
insistent, and her senses skyrocketed. She opened
to him and wound her arms around his neck, her
body pressing against the hard planes of his frame.

His tongue met hers in a silken thrust that set off
fireworks in her blood. Molten heat flared in her
core and her legs trembled with the effort of keeping upright. He made a rough sound at the back of
his throat and brought her even closer, one of his
hands pressed against the curve of her bottom, the
other buried in the tresses of her hair. The slight
tether of his fingers in her hair felt almost primal,
possessive, and a shiver coursed down her spine like
a shower of champagne bubbles. Louis angled his
head to change position, deepening the kiss even

further. An intense ache spread through her flesh, centred in her core where a heavy pulse thrummed.

He lifted his mouth off hers, his breathing heavy, his eyes glinting with desire. 'Hold that thought, *ma chérie.* I'd better not be late for my mother's birthday dinner. I'll finish this in Paris.'

'Is that a promise?'

He smiled a sexy smile that made her inner core shiver in anticipation. 'Damn right it is.'

'So, Paris this week with Louis, huh?' Millie said, watching Ivy pack her bag in her bedroom later that evening. 'What happened to the one-night-only rule? Who changed it? You or him?'

Ivy folded a silk evening blouse and placed it in her bag on the bed. 'He did.'

'Woo-hoo. You go, girl. You must have some serious chemistry going on between you.'

Ivy put a matching skirt next to the blouse in her bag. 'It's just a fling, Millie. Don't get too excited. He's not the falling in love type.'

'Maybe not, but you definitely are. Are you sure you're not falling a teensy weensy bit in love with him?' Millie pressed her thumb and index finger together in a tiny pinching gesture.

'It would be crazy for me to develop feelings for him.' Crazy, crazy, crazy—so she had to try even harder to ignore those soft little flutters in her heart every time he looked at her.

Millie picked up a pendant she'd designed for Ivy's last birthday and ran the fine silver chain through her fingers. 'Let me know if you want me to design your engagement and wedding rings for you. Mates' rates and all.' Her friend might not be able to keep a secret, but she was excellent at spotting a white lie when she heard one.

Ivy turned to pick out some underwear from the wardrobe. 'Don't be silly. There's not going to be an engagement or wedding. We're calling it quits after Paris.'

She gripped the edge of the drawer and tried to imagine going back to being friends with Louis instead of lovers. How would she be able to do it? How could she look at him and not think of how it felt to be in his arms? To have his mouth clamped to hers, his body buried deep inside her? To feel the stroke of his hand down her spine or to feel his arm slip around her waist and draw her closer? Her body literally ached when she wasn't with him. She had relived his love-making hundreds of times since coming home from work that evening. Her body was still humming and thrumming with the need he awakened.

Millie put down the pendant and met Ivy's gaze. 'But you don't want it to end it, do you?'

Ivy sat on the bed with a sigh. 'No. Not yet.'

Millie sat beside her and slipped an arm around her shoulders. 'I won't tell you I told you so.'

Ivy gave her the side-eye. 'Thanks.'

'I'll save that phrase for my mother. Did I tell you she's getting divorced again?'

'Again? How many times is that? Three?'

Millie flicked her eyes upwards in a despairing manner. 'Four. And each time she's been royally screwed over.' She bounced off the bed and turned to face Ivy, her expression determined. 'I'm not going to watch her get done over again. I'm saving up to get the best lawyer for her I can.'

'They don't come cheap. What about asking the guy you went on that blind date with a couple of months ago... Hunter Addison? Isn't he a celebrity divorce lawyer? I've heard he's brilliant. He might do it pro bono for you. It can't hurt to ask him.'

Millie's cheeks went as pink as the silk shirt in Ivy's weekend bag. 'Erm...well... I kind of burned my boats with him.'

'Oh, really? What happened that night? You've always been a little cagey about talking about it.'

Millie shrugged one shoulder in an off-hand manner. 'Nothing happened other than we both decided our mutual friends got it wrong in thinking we might ever hit it off. We had nothing in common and spent the whole ghastly evening annoying each other.'

Ivy wondered if her friend had deliberately sabotaged the date out of her unwillingness to move on from the death of her fiancé. 'Hmm, well, all I can say is, he might be the worst blind date but word has it he's one of the best divorce lawyers in London. If you don't get him for your mum, then her ex will get him and, believe you me, you don't want the best in the business working for your enemy.'

Millie chewed at the corner of her mouth; her eyes were troubled. 'Gosh, I hadn't thought of it that way…' She straightened her shoulders and painted a bright smile on her face that didn't fool Ivy for a second. 'I'd better let you finish packing. Enjoy Paris.'

'I will.'

It didn't matter where she went with Louis, it would be impossible not to enjoy herself. The only trouble was…what would she have after Paris?

Memories. That was all.

CHAPTER SEVEN

THEY FLEW TO PARIS the following morning and a short time afterwards Louis took her to his apartment in the Sixteenth Arrondissement in Saint-Germain-des-Prés. The historic architecture was stunning, and many of the beautiful old buildings had been turned into modern apartments—including Louis'.

Ivy stepped over the threshold and stood for a moment, struck speechless by the elegance and design. The crystal chandeliers overhead tinkled from the slight draught from the door opening and closing. The marble floor was covered in places with hand-woven silk rugs that were so soft to step on, she thought her ankles were going to be swallowed. The pieces of antique furniture were priceless and came from various periods—from as early as the Renaissance, through to Louis XIV, Louis XV, Regency, Art Deco and Art Nouveau to modern times.

'Oh, my God.' She stepped further into the foyer, touching various pieces with worshipful fingers.

'Your taste is amazing. And your budget. Some of these things must've cost a fortune.'

'If I like something, I buy it. I don't allow the expense to influence my decision.'

'Lucky you.' Ivy leaned down to look more closely at a Louis XV rosewood and gold-inlaid writing desk she was sure she had seen before at work. 'Hey, I'm sure we had this piece in the show room last year. I seem to remember a French interior designer bought it with a whole shipment of other stuff.' She straightened and looked at Louis. 'Did she buy it on your behalf?'

His expression was indecipherable. 'I told her to buy from your shop because I know you have good quality, genuine antiques.'

Ivy gave a rueful smile. 'It's not my shop, it's Mr Thornley's and I have a horrible feeling he's going to sell it now that his wife's health is going downhill.'

'Would you like to own your own business rather than work for someone else?'

Ivy ran a lazy finger over the gold inlay on the writing desk. 'I don't know… I want to keep working in antiques, but I want to have a family one day, and running a business is hard work and very time-consuming.' She lowered her hand from the table and glanced at him. 'And I certainly don't have the money to buy Mr Thornley's business. Not with Mum needing financial top-ups all the time.'

A frown settled on his brow. 'Your mother's financial problems are not your responsibility.'

She gave him an ironic look. 'And nor are they yours, but you still bail her out from time to time.'

He gave a crooked smile. *'Touché.'* His smile faded and he continued, 'But it's hard not to feel sorry for her. She's never really got over your father leaving, has she?'

Ivy shook her head and sighed. 'No. They were childhood sweethearts. He was her first lover. She thought they'd be together forever and then he traded her in for someone half her age.'

'Marriage doesn't suit all men.'

Ivy had come to realise, since sleeping with Louis, how much her mother's lifestyle choices had affected her while growing up. The fear of being rejected by someone you thought loved you was too terrifying.

'Remember how I told you how my mother was so out of control with her drinking and flings with men she'd met at the pub? Well, it embarrassed me so much, and I think it's why I locked down my own budding sexuality. Mum was so open about sex that it made me all the more uncomfortable. She would talk about her latest lover and what they'd got up to and I'd cringe with embarrassment. *I* became the disapproving, prudish parent rather than the young teenage girl I really was.

'And I couldn't talk to Dad about it, because it

might have made him fight for full custody, and no way did I want to live with him and his younger girlfriend. I'd then have to watch him acting like a born-again teenager with her every day instead of only the occasional weekend. And I didn't want to worry Ronan because he was having enough trouble dealing with his own issues. I'm sure he would have come out about his sexuality a whole lot sooner if it hadn't been for my parents breaking up and carrying on the way they did.'

Louis squeezed both her hands. 'You've both done an amazing job of surviving what was and still is a difficult time. Parents can be so annoying when they let us down. But we let them down too, I guess. And those of us who choose to be parents will one day do the same to their children.'

Ivy tilted her head at him. 'Have you ever been unfaithful to a partner?'

'I'm never with them long enough to think of straying.'

'But would you, if you were?'

'No.' There was a firm edge of finality about his tone. 'An affair hurts everyone in the end. No one wins. I admire people who can move on from it but I'm not sure I could.'

'Nor me. It's a deal breaker for me. One of my flatmates, Zoey, was cheated on by a long-term boyfriend over a year ago. She's still not over it.'

Louis picked up their bags from where he'd left

them on the floor. 'I'll take these upstairs. Have you got to be somewhere by a certain time?'

'This afternoon I have to meet with the daughter of the man who died at the villa in Montmartre, where the deceased estate is being housed. Mr Thornley wants me to check the quality and authenticity of the Victorian china before we commit to buying anything.'

'Have you got time for a quick lunch?'

Ivy glanced at her watch. 'Sure. But don't you have meetings too?'

'They can wait.'

A short time later, Louis took Ivy to one of the cafés nearby. He watched her work her way through a crispy baguette and soft, creamy cheese, marinated olives and a glass of white wine, her enjoyment obvious with the little 'Mmm' sounds she made. She caught him looking at her and her cheeks turned a light shade of pink. 'Why are you looking at me like that? Haven't you seen a woman eat before?'

Louis smiled and reached for his barely touched wine. 'It is indeed a rare occurrence for me to be with a woman who really enjoys her food.'

'That'll teach you for dating supermodels all the time.' She picked up another olive and popped it in her mouth. She chewed and swallowed, then added, 'I forgot to ask you how your mother's birthday dinner went.'

He took a slow sip of wine before answering. 'It was...bearable.' He put his glass back on the table and leaned back in his seat. 'At least they didn't bicker the whole time I was there.'

Ivy grimaced. 'If they're so unhappy, why do they stay together? Surely it would be better to call it quits or get counselling or something?'

'They were happy once.' Louis leaned forward to take a couple of olives off the plate between them. He put them on his side plate and then wiped his fingers on his napkin. Talking about his parents always ruined his appetite. 'But my mother's disappointment at not being able to give my father the large family he wanted ate away at that happiness.'

'That's so sad. But at least your dad didn't trade your mum in for someone who could give him what he wanted. That's something to be grateful for, I guess.'

Louis' mind flashed back to his mother's blank face and deadened personality while she'd been in the mental health clinic. His gut—even after all this time—tightened into hard knots and his skin went ice-cold. 'Yes, that's true.'

Ivy leaned forward across the table and placed her hand on his wrist. 'What's wrong?'

Louis rearranged his features into a blank mask. 'Nothing, why?'

She leaned back and sighed. 'I don't know...it

just looked like you were really upset about something but trying not to show it.'

He must be slipping. He had no idea he had become so transparent. Another good reason only to spend this week with her before she got even further under his guard. 'Talking about my parents isn't my favourite pastime.'

She looked at him for a long moment. 'You care about them, don't you? Even though they are difficult and annoying, deep down you love them, otherwise you wouldn't make time for your mother's birthday.'

Louis picked up his wine glass again. 'You're becoming quite the little psychologist, aren't you?' He kept his tone playful and accompanied it with an indolent smile.

She twitched her nose in her cute bunny way. 'I'm always banging on about my parents, but I really love Mum. Dad, not so much. I guess I've taught myself not to care any more about him. It's less painful.'

Louis waited a beat before responding, 'My father suggested separating to my mother when I was ten years old, but she had a mental health crisis as a result. A serious one. She ended up in a clinic for months. He has never mentioned the words separation or divorce since in case she took another overdose.'

Ivy blinked at him in shock. 'Oh, I'm so sorry. How terribly distressing.'

Louis flicked a baguette crumb off the table with his fingers. 'I used to hate going to see her at the clinic. I don't know if it was the heavy drugs the doctors gave her, or whether she had completely shut down, but she was blank and motionless, just a body lying on the bed. She didn't talk, she didn't smile, she didn't even seem to know who I was most days.'

Ivy reached forward again and grasped his hand. 'Oh, Louis, how frightened and confused you must have been. Does Ronan know about this? He's never said anything.'

'No, I didn't tell him. It's not something I ever talk about with anyone.' He gave a rueful twist of his mouth. 'It happened a long time ago. I've almost forgotten about it now.' Almost. But every now and again his mother would get a vacant look in her eyes and a wave of dread would swamp him. Was it happening again? Was she thinking of taking another overdose? The torturous thoughts circled his brain for hours as he remembered the anguish he'd felt and his utter powerlessness at being unable to do anything to help her.

'I'm not sure anyone could forget such a harrowing time,' Ivy said, softly stroking the back of his hand. 'Has she ever had a relapse?'

'Thankfully, no.'

'But you must be living in dread of it anyway.' Her insight was spot on, which shouldn't have surprised him. But he wasn't used to being close enough to a person for them to see the structural cracks in his façade. His childhood foundation had been compromised like a building that had suffered a destabilising earthquake tremor. He had reinforced where he could but there were still hairline cracks if you looked close enough. And he had a feeling Ivy was looking very closely indeed. Too close for comfort.

Louis glanced pointedly at his watch. 'I hate to break up the true confessions party, but I have to see a man about a house.'

Ivy pulled her hand away from his and looked at the time on her phone. 'Goodness, is that the time? I've got to dash too.'

Louis rose from the table to help her with her chair, resisting the almost uncontrollable urge to turn her in his arms and kiss her. He breathed in the fragrance of her perfume instead. But then she turned around, stepped up on tiptoe and brushed his lips with hers in a soft kiss that sent a shudder of longing through him.

'Thanks for lunch. And thanks for telling me about your childhood. I know it was hard for you to do so.'

She knew way too much but, strangely, it didn't bother him as much as he thought it would. A weight had come off him in revealing his childhood drama. A weight he hadn't even been conscious of carrying. He brushed a wayward strand of hair away from her face, his chest feeling as soft and mushy as the creamy Camembert on the table.

'*De rien.* You're welcome. I'll book somewhere nice for dinner.' He leaned down and kissed her on both cheeks, and then on the plump cushion of her mouth. '*Au revoir, ma chèrie.*'

She clutched at her chest in a pretend swoon. 'If you're going to speak French to me the whole time we're here, I'll melt into a puddle at your feet.'

Louis smiled and playfully touched her cheek with his finger. 'I hope your meeting goes well.' He reached into his trouser pocket and handed her the spare key to his apartment. There was another first for him—he had never given anyone a key to his apartment before. He was crossing a line he had never crossed before, but he reassured himself it was only for five days. 'I'm not sure how long I'll be, so just make your way home and I'll meet you there.'

'Okay.' She took the key and popped it in her bag, snapping it shut with a resounding click. Her eyes were clear and bright as she met his gaze. 'Louis?'

'Yes?'

'Thank you for asking me to come with you to Paris. I was kind of dreading coming on my own.'

He leaned down and pressed another kiss to her lips. 'I was too.'

On her way home from her appointment Ivy was still ruminating over Louis' revelation about his mother's breakdown. It explained so much about his guardedness with relationships. The fear he must have felt over seeing his mother in such a state, not to mention the suicide attempt itself. It was a lot to handle for a child of ten, especially a deeply sensitive and intuitive one like Louis.

Until recently, Ivy hadn't realised how truly sensitive he was, but as she had come to know him better she could see how it had played an important and significant role in helping her brother Ronan finally gain the courage to come out as gay. Louis had been the steady, stable friend who had never once wavered in his support.

And he had sent her a gorgeous bouquet of flowers after her elderly dog Fergus had died, understanding how devastated she was at losing her beloved pet.

He had been sensitive to her mother's financial issues, taking it upon himself to give her a loan that Ivy knew for a fact he wouldn't want to be repaid.

How could she stop her admiration for him turning into something bigger, broader, more consuming than a simple friendship? It had happened almost without her realising it.

Louis wasn't incapable of love. She could sense the deep care and concern he had for his parents even though it was tempered by his frustration with them. He resisted long-term love out of fear, just as she had resisted dating and becoming intimate with someone in case they hurt her, like her mother had been hurt. Like she had been hurt when her father had claimed to love her and yet abandoned her because of her loyalty to Ronan.

Of course there was a risk she would get hurt by Louis. But didn't all relationships carry some element of risk? Even Millie and Zoey let her down occasionally, as she did them. It was part of the deal with caring about people—investing in their lives, sharing the highs and lows and everything in between.

But Louis was only offering her five days in Paris. He wasn't offering forever. He wasn't offering her the fairy tale she longed for.

Five days.

How could she have thought it would ever be enough?

CHAPTER EIGHT

LOUIS MET WITH a couple of clients in his Paris office, as well as catching up with two of the junior architects he was mentoring, but the whole time his thoughts kept drifting to Ivy. Just knowing she would be waiting at home for him made his body tingle in anticipation. He wished now he hadn't promised to take her out to dinner. He would much prefer to have had a simple meal at home and make love to her for hours. He wanted this week to be special for her, a time she could look back on with pleasure instead of regret.

If anyone had told him a few days ago he would ask her to be with him for five days in Paris, he would have laughed out loud. But, ever since the Saturday morning when he'd woken to find her gone from his Cotswold house, he had been obsessed with spending more time with her. His work was taking a back seat when usually it was front and centre. His mind was full of images of her beautiful body, his desire for her a constant background ache that tortured him relentlessly.

But it wasn't only the physical attraction that drew him to her. She was open emotionally, he was closed, and yet somehow he felt drawn to revealing more of himself to her. Telling her—telling *anyone*—about his childhood would have been unthinkable, even days ago. But revealing his pain over his mother's breakdown had released a tight knot inside him. A knot that had formed when he'd been ten years old and never once eased its tension.

He had never been a fan of talk therapy—what words could ever undo things that had been done? Things he had witnessed and never wanted to see again? But somehow Ivy's gentle empathy had soothed a raw ache in his heart, like a cooling salve does to a scalding burn. His body was hungry for her touch in a way it had never been for anyone else's.

There was a corner of his mind that raised a red flag. One day someone else's touch would have to satisfy him because he wasn't prepared to risk falling in love with her. His parents had once been in love, madly in love, yet they had done nothing more than make each other miserable since.

He couldn't bear the thought of Ivy one day looking at him or speaking to him the way his mother did to his father. So few long-term relationships lasted the distance with both parties happy and contented. Why would he think he and Ivy had a

chance? He had never been good at romantic relationships. He got bored so quickly. Desire flared
and then just as quickly faded.

But so far it hadn't faded with Ivy. In fact, it was
flaring and flashing and firing all the time. He only
had to stand next to her for his blood to pound. He only
had to touch her and his senses went wild. He only had
to kiss her for a tsunami of lust to blast through him.

Louis walked back to his apartment and stopped
on the way to buy flowers and some chocolates from
a specialty chocolatier. But then he walked past a
jewellery store and found himself turning back to
have a look in the window. Sparkling diamonds,
midnight-blue sapphires, blood-red rubies, forest-
green emeralds and milky-white pearls were displayed in a glorious array.

And then his eye caught sight of a rare pink Ar-
gyle diamond from the Kimberley region of Australia. The pink hue reminded him of Ivy's cheeks
when she blushed.

*You're thinking of buying her jewellery? A dia-
mond? Seriously?*

Louis ignored the voice in his head and listened
to the one in his heart. It was her thirtieth birthday soon and he wanted to buy something special
for her. It was an early birthday gift. Nothing else.

When Ivy got back to Louis' apartment, she expected to find her luggage in one of the spare bed-

rooms but instead found it in the master suite. Did that mean he intended to spend the whole night with her? Or maybe it was because he didn't trust her to disappear again without saying goodbye.

She opened her bag and began unpacking her things, feeling a little awkward about hanging her clothes next to his in the walk-in wardrobe. But she didn't want to drape her clothes over the back of a chair or dressing table and, as they would be in Paris for five days, what else was she supposed to do?

She found some spare coat hangers and hung her clothes on the opposite side of his. He had an assortment of expensively tailored suits and crisp shirts, ties, Italian leather shoes and belts, and cufflinks in a glass-topped drawer. There were casual clothes as well—jeans, shirts and T-shirts, shorts and leather loafers. She found herself trailing her hand along his clothes, breathing in the faint trace of his aftershave and the smell that was unique to him.

'Have you found enough space for your things?' Louis' deep voice spoke from the door of the walk-in wardrobe and Ivy jumped and spun round, her cheeks feeling hot enough to iron her clothes.

'I wasn't sure if you wanted me to sleep in the spare room or—'

'I want you with me.' His eyes were dark—more inky-black pupils than grey-blue irises. They drifted to her mouth and back again in a slow perusal and a frisson passed over her flesh.

'So you can stop me running away without saying goodbye?'

He came closer, placing his hands on her hips and shifting her so she was flush against his body. The possessive warmth of his hands sent a flare of molten heat to her core and the unmistakable jut of his erection sent her heart rate soaring. His thighs were like columns of steel, while hers felt like soggy noodles as desire shuddered through her body. 'I'll have to find a way to entice you to stay with me.' His tone was deep, smoky, sexy, and another delicate shiver coursed down her spine.

Ivy stood on tiptoe and placed her arms around his neck, the elevation in height bringing her breasts into closer contact with his rock-hard chest. She gave him a playful look. 'I wonder how you'll do that? I'm not easily enticed.'

He glided his hands up from her hips to her ribcage, close to her breasts but not touching them. The desire to have him do so was a tingling ache that was both pleasure and pain. His gaze went to her mouth, his lips tipped up at the corners in a slow smile that heated her blood to boiling.

'And I'm not easily bewitched but somehow you've achieved it.'

His mouth came down to hers in an explosive kiss that sent a shockwave of lust through her body. She opened to the demanding thrust of his tongue, relishing the erotic play that made her tingle from head to foot. His lips were firm yet gentle, teasing her into a response that was almost feverish. She gasped, she whimpered, she clung to him, desperate to take in more of him. He tasted of mint and male heat and mad passion and she couldn't get enough. His kiss was like a drug to her senses, sending her into a frenzy of need that spiralled through every inch of her flesh. Her most intimate flesh swelled with blood, moistened with excitement, lava-hot and hungry for his possession.

He lifted his mouth off hers, gazing at her with glittering eyes. His hands moved up to cup her breasts through her clothes and she gave another desperate whimper. 'Let's get these clothes off you, shall we?'

'Do let's.' Ivy began to unbutton her top, but her fingers wouldn't cooperate, so he took over. Slowly, torturously slowly, leaving a kiss on each section of her skin as he exposed it.

'Your skin tastes so good.' His voice was deep and rough, his lips warm and sending sparks of heat to her core. He peeled off her blouse and bent his head to her breasts, still encased in a balcony bra. He gave each upper curve a lazy lion-like lick that made her gasp with pleasure. He deftly unclipped the fastening on her bra and it fell in a silky silence to the floor. He drew in a shuddering breath and stroked his tongue over and around her right nipple, then he gently sucked on her, drawing her into the heat of his mouth. He released her nipple and then ever so lightly took it between his teeth. The soft tether of his teeth to her sensitive flesh sent a wave of tingly warmth through her pelvis.

Ivy clutched at his head, arching her spine, her body raging with need. 'I want you. Now.'

Louis straightened and gave her a slow smile. 'I like hearing you beg. It turns me on.'

Ivy shivered at the dark glint in his gaze. She tugged at his shirt, pulling it out of his trousers, and began to undo the buttons with more haste than competence. A button popped off and landed nearby. 'Let's even this up a bit. I'm not going to bare all unless you get naked too.'

'Good plan.' He shrugged off his shirt but left her to undo the waistband of his trousers, sucking in a breath when her fingers skated over his erection. 'Your touch drives me crazy.' He stepped out of his trousers and underwear and came back to work on the rest of her clothes, unzipping her skirt and peeling away her knickers. He feasted his eyes on her naked body, making her feel like the most beautiful and sexy woman on the planet. 'Everything about you drives me crazy.'

'Right back at you,' Ivy said, barely able to speak for the sensations rushing through her body. Urgent needs begged to be assuaged. Needs she'd had no idea she possessed until his touch had awakened her.

Louis scooped her up and carried her out of the

walk-in wardrobe to his bed, laying her down before joining her. He glided one of his hands down from the top of her shoulder, over her breast and ribcage, over her stomach and lower abdomen, down the flank of her thigh and then back up again. A slow, sensuous glide that made her aware of every millimetre of her skin, every pore responding to his touch, every nerve tingling. His eyes drank in every curve of her body, making her feel utterly feminine and desirable.

'So, so beautiful—every part of you.' His voice had an almost reverential note to it, and it made it all the harder to ignore the way her feelings for him had intensified. Going from a platonic admiration to full-blown passionate adoration—a mature and lasting adoration that she had longed to feel for someone all her life.

Ivy placed her hand on the side of his face, enjoying the masculine texture of his skin so different from her own. 'You make me feel beautiful…' Her voice caught on the words, so intense were her emotions. She didn't want to spoil the moment by blurting out her feelings. They weren't part of their arrangement. But holding them in, keeping them hidden, made her heart ache with the pressure of keeping them contained. She spoke them with her hands instead, stroking each of his eyebrows, down the length of his nose, around his mouth.

He brought his mouth down to hers, kissing her

deeply, lingeringly, his tongue playing with hers in a dance as old as time itself. A primal dance, erotic and playful, yet with deadly serious intent. His intention was clear—she felt it in every stroke of his tongue, every glide of his hand, every erogenous zone he touched. He wanted her. He was going to have her. She would enjoy every heart-stopping second of it.

Ivy breathed in the scent of him, the musk and salt and aroused male smell that so tantalised her senses. He lifted his mouth off hers to work his way down her body, leaving branding kisses that sent her pulse skyrocketing. He went from her breasts to her belly and beyond, her skin tightening in anticipation. He parted her with his fingers, exploring her most intimate flesh with his lips and tongue. The tension gathered in her swollen tissues, a delicious tension that built to a crescendo. And then the storm broke and she was flying, falling, swirling and spinning in a vortex of intense, spine-tingling pleasure, the ripples and aftershocks spreading throughout her pelvis. 'Oh, wow…oh, wow…oh, wow…' Her breaths came in stuttering gasps, her limbs feeling spent and useless.

Louis kissed his way back up her body, holding her gaze when he got close to her mouth. 'I love watching you come. You hold nothing back.'

Ivy was holding far more back than he realised. Love flowed through her as passionately as her orgasm had just done. She could feel it fill every part of her being, a deep attachment to him that was going to be hard to ignore for much longer. But how could she tell him? It wasn't something he wanted to hear from her. It wasn't something he wanted to hear from anyone. He'd been a playboy for a long time, and he would go back to being one once their fling was over.

Her heart contracted at the thought of him moving between lovers in the future. One after the other, each one a fleeting encounter that meant nothing more than a temporary relief of lust. And back in her normal day-to-day life she would be grieving the loss of his intimate touch, mourning the end of their passionate fling. How would she bear it? She ran her fingertip over his sensual bottom lip, her gaze carefully avoiding his. 'I hope I can be just as responsive with someone else when the time comes.'

The silence thrummed with an unusual energy as if each and every oxygen particle had been disturbed by her comment. Even *she* was disturbed by her comment. How could she ever make love with someone else? Who would make her flesh sing the way Louis did? It was unthinkable. Impossible.

By the time Ivy brought her gaze back to his, Louis' expression was masked, all except for a camera-shutter-quick movement at the back of his gaze. No more than a rapid blink—a reset, an unwelcome thought swiftly, ruthlessly blocked. 'I seem to remember I promised to take you out to dinner, but I got a little waylaid.' His tone was mildly playful but it was at odds with his screened features.

Ivy stroked her hand down his lean jaw, one of her legs hooking over his. 'How can you think of food at a time like this?'

His mouth came down to just above hers. 'Believe me, *ma chérie*, I am definitely not thinking of food right now. I'm only hungry for you.' His kiss showed her just how hungry, his hands urgently moving over her body even more so.

Ivy pressed herself closer, drawn to the heat and power of his hard male body, her smooth legs entwined with his hair-roughened ones, her body on fire. He moved away only long enough to get a condom and she watched him smooth it over himself, her pulse racing with excitement, her inner core heated with longing. He positioned himself over her, balancing his weight so as not to overpower her, his entry swift, sensual, sense-spinning. Tingles shot through her sensitive tissues, her body gripping him, welcoming him, pleasuring him as his pleasured her. His guttural groans were music to her ears, his deep, rhythmic thrusts ramping up the coil of tension in her core. She was climbing a mountain, higher, higher, the pinnacle just out of reach. She wanted. She wanted. She wanted. The aching throb in her body was accompanied by the chant in her head.

'Please…please…*please*…' She didn't care that she was begging. She didn't care that she was thrashing beneath him like a paper boat in a storm-tossed sea.

'Come for me.' Louis' voice was husky. 'Don't hold back. Don't be frightened of it. Let it take you.'

He slipped his hand between their bodies and slowly caressed her moist and swollen flesh. The delicious sensations came from far-off places in her body, gathering to a feverish point in her female centre. And then they exploded in a shower of sparks and tingles and spasms that carried her to another plane of existence. An exquisite existence of sheer mind-blowing, planet-shifting ecstasy. It was bigger and better than anything she had experienced before, the monumental force of it almost terrifying. How could her body split from her mind in such a way? How could her body contain so many nerve endings? So many pleasurable settings that fired with such heart-stopping intensity?

Louis kept moving within her, taking his own pleasure with deep thrusts and guttural groans until, finally, he tensed all over and then gave one last shuddering groan as his orgasm hit. Ivy held him through the storm, feeling completely undone by the way his body responded to hers. So powerful, so potent, so primal and passionate. She moved her hands up and down his back in smooth massaging movements, listening to his breathing quietening, enjoying the relaxed weight of him lying over her.

'Am I too heavy for you?' His lips moved against the sensitive skin of her neck where his head was buried, and she shivered.

'No...' She gave a long blissful sigh and stroked her hand over the taut shape of his buttocks. 'If anyone had said a few weeks ago I'd feel comfortable with a naked man sprawled over me after making mad, passionate love to me, I would have laughed. Or fainted.'

He leaned up on one elbow, a smile tilting one side of his mouth, his eyes dark and lustrous. He traced his finger from her chin to her sternum and then back to her lower lip, teasing it with a feather-light caress. 'It's good you feel comfortable with me.' His smile slowly faded and his gaze grew serious. 'But neither of us can get too comfortable with this arrangement. The time limit still stands.'

Ivy had to work hard not to show her disappointment. She was conscious of her every facial muscle, of trying to control the micro-expressions that might betray her emotions.

The time limit still stands.

He wasn't budging from his rules on their fling. In spite of the fabulous sex, in spite of their friendship and the increasing closeness she felt was growing between them, he was determined to keep things temporary.

'I know.' She gave a little forced laugh. 'Just think what Ronan would say if he knew we were having a fling. Or Mum.'

The frown between his eyebrows deepened. 'Yes, well, all the more reason to stick to the rules. I don't want anyone's expectations raised and then dashed when our…fling ends.'

His slight hesitation over the word 'fling' made her wonder if perhaps a part of him—a secret, well-buried part—was already compartmentalising his involvement with her as something completely different from his normal flings. He rolled away from her, got off the bed and disposed of the condom in the bathroom.

Ivy used the opportunity while he was in the bathroom to wrap herself in a plush bathrobe. His bathrobe that contained the tantalising scent of him on its soft fibres. It completely swamped her, but at least it covered her nakedness. But it wasn't really her physical nakedness she was most worried about covering—it was her emotional nakedness. The raw hope filling her heart more and more each day that he would come to love her. A hope that refused to give up even though it was hanging by a silken thread.

She desperately hoped he would want more than a scratch-an-itch fling. That the chemistry between them would prove to him that what they'd experienced together was special, unique, something to be treasured and not put aside as a distant memory.

Louis disposed of the condom and gripped the edge of the basin in front of the mirror. He looked at his reflection and wasn't sure he liked what he saw. A man who was seriously questioning if he'd done the right thing in sleeping with Ivy. Not because he didn't enjoy every moment of having her in his arms—he did. Too much. Way too much. So much, he was finding it harder and harder to think of their involvement as a fling. As a casual fling, like any other he'd experienced. It wasn't and it could never be. It was in an entirely different category. Not just because he was her first lover. Not just because the sex was so fulfilling and mind-blowingly pleasurable and made his body hum for hours afterwards. But because it was Ivy. Sweet, cute, adorable Ivy, with her dimples and her curls and her curves and her funny little bunny twitch.

But one day, in the not too distant future he would have to see Ivy move on with someone else. Someone who would give her the things she wanted— love, marriage, babies, commitment for a lifetime. And she had every right to want those things. She deserved no less than wholehearted commitment and love.

His gut twisted like writhing snakes. One day, he would even have to attend her wedding or think of a very good excuse not to accept the invitation, thus hurting her, her mother and her brother in one fell swoop. God, how had he got himself into this mess? A beautiful mess he didn't want to end.

Not yet.

CHAPTER NINE

Ivy WANDERED OUT to the salon, still dressed in Louis' bathrobe, where there was a huge bunch of pink roses wrapped in white paper and tied with a black satin bow resting on the coffee table. There was a box of chocolates from a Parisian chocolatier next to them, as well as a flat, rectangular black velvet jewellery box.

Her breath stalled, her heart tripped, her stomach flipped. Flowers. Chocolates. Jewellery. Gifts a man in love gave to the woman he adored. Hope spread throughout her chest, lifting her spirits, sending a burst of happiness through her.

But then a doubt slipped into her mind like a curl of toxic smoke wafting under a door, slowly but surely poisoning her fledgling hopes. For all she knew, he might buy all his lovers gifts. Consolation prizes, trinkets to remember him by when their fling came to its inevitable end.

She wanted more than memories. She had been

trying to ignore it from the first time he'd kissed her, but she could ignore it no longer. Her love for him had been in the background for so long, she hadn't recognised it until it had moved to centre stage. The passion he awakened in her had turned a spotlight on her emotions. Emotions she had shied away from at first, keeping them in the shadows in case she got hurt. But they were out of the shadows now, spreading light over all her self-delusions, revealing the truth at the heart of her involvement with Louis. She loved him. She wanted him, not just during a fling, but forever.

Louis came out from the bedroom and she turned to face him. He was still naked, apart from a white towel wrapped around his lean hips, and his hair looked as if it had been recently combed with his fingers.

'Are these for me?' She pointed to the items on the coffee table, keeping her expression neutral... Well, as neutral as she could, which wasn't saying much.

'Who else would they be for?' His tone was guarded, as if he sensed the undercurrent of tension in her face and body that she was so desperately trying to hide.

Ivy turned back to the coffee table and leaned down to pick up the roses, lifting them to her face to breathe in the sweet fragrance. She put them back on the table and turned sideways to look at him again. 'You don't have to buy me gifts, Louis. You've spent enough money helping my mother without going to any more expense on me as well.'

He came further into the room to stand on the other side of the coffee table. 'I have plenty of money, and if I want to spend it I will.' His tone had a clipped edge, as if he was annoyed at her attitude to his generosity.

Ivy elevated her chin, locking her gaze on his inscrutable one. 'I don't want you buying me hideously expensive gifts. I don't need compensation for when our…fling is over.'

A savage frown divided his brow. 'Compensation? Is that what you think this is?' He waved a hand at the gifts on the table between them, his grey-blue eyes glittering with something that very much looked like anger. Good, because she was angry too. Furiously angry that he was paying her off. Softening the blow with fancy gifts when all she wanted was his love. Not his money, just his love.

Ivy arched her eyebrows in a haughty manner. 'Isn't it?'

He muttered a swear word in both French and English, his hand reaching up to rub the back of his neck, as if to relieve sudden tension. He dropped his hand back by his side, every muscle in his body rigid. Unyielding. As though he was putting up a physical barrier as impenetrable as his emotional firewall.

'No. It is not that at all.' Each word was bitten out, his mouth set in a tight line. 'The flowers and chocolates are to thank you for coming with me to Paris. The jewellery is for your birthday—I thought I'd give it to you early in case I don't see you on the day. If you want to read anything else into it, then fine, go right ahead.'

Ivy's anger deflated like a pricked party balloon. 'Oh, Louis, I'm sorry. I almost forgot about my birthday.' He had made her forget everything but how wonderful it was to be in his arms. And how, within a matter of four impossibly short days, she would be out of them and alone again.

He shrugged one broad shoulder in a dismissive manner. 'Forget about it.' His tone was gruff, offhand, but she could read a thread of lingering hurt in it too.

She stepped around the coffee table and placed her hand on his leanly muscled forearm, meshing her gaze with his screened one. 'I'm sorry for being tetchy when you've been so generous. Forgive me?'

He made a soft grunting sound and wrapped his arms around her and brought her close against him, his head resting on the top of her head. 'There's nothing to forgive.' His deep voice reverberated against her cheek where it was resting against his broad chest. She wanted to stay there forever, just like this, in the warm, protective shelter of his arms.

After a long moment, Ivy tilted her head back to look at him. 'Can I open my present now?'

He smiled and gave her bottom a playful pat. 'Go for it.'

She slipped out of his arms to pick up the jewellery box, holding her breath as she flicked the little gold latch and opened the lid. Lying on a cream velvet bed was a pink diamond pendant on an exquisitely fine white-gold chain with a matching pair of droplet earrings. 'Oh, my goodness…' She stared at them in amazement, struck by their beauty and his thoughtfulness. 'They're just divine. Thank you so much.'

'Do you want to try them on?'

She gave him a rueful smile. 'I'm not sure they'll be shown off to their best advantage while I'm wearing your bathrobe, as expensive and luxurious as it is.'

His grey-blue eyes smouldered. 'There's an easy solution to that.'

He reached for the waist ties of the bathrobe and slowly, deliberately, untied them, all the while holding her gaze in an unwavering lock. Then he slipped the bathrobe off her shoulders, his eyes hungrily travelling over her naked flesh. The garment fell to the floor at her feet and he took the jewellery box from her.

'Turn around.' His commanding tone made a shiver run up and down her spine, so too the brush of his fingers as he fastened the pendant around her neck. He placed a warm, firm hand on one of her shoulders to turn her back round. 'You'd better put the earrings on yourself.'

He handed them to her and she slipped them through her pierced earlobes. 'How do I look?'

His gaze swept over her again. 'Ravishing.' He placed his hands on her hips and brought her up against him. She was left in no doubt of how ravishing he found her—he was as hard as stone—and her lower body responded with hot little flickers of lust. He brought his mouth down to hers in an incendiary kiss that set off fireworks and bombs in her blood. Heat raced through her system, molten heat that made every cell in her body throb and ache with rampaging need. He deepened the kiss with a silken thrust of his tongue, calling hers into intimate play, teasing, cajoling, captivating her senses until she was whimpering with delight.

Somehow his towel fell to the floor, but she couldn't remember if she'd tugged it off or he had. All that mattered was it was off, and she could feel him rising against her belly, the velvet and steel of his form inciting her to even greater dizzying heights of arousal. Her body was slick, her legs trembling, her spine loosening.

'I want you so damn much.' He growled against her lips, his hands moving from her hips to cup her breasts. He brought his mouth to each breast in turn, licking and circling each tightly budded nipple with his tongue. The sensations rioted from her breasts throughout her body on intricate networks of sheer pleasure.

Ivy grasped his head in her hands, bringing his mouth back to hers. 'I want you too. So much it's like a pain.'

His eyes gleamed with erotic promise, his lips tilted in a smile that sent another wave of heat through to her core. 'Then let's do something about that, shall we?' He picked her up and carried her back to the bedroom, placing her on the bed and coming down beside her.

Ivy waited with bated breath as he reached past her to get a condom. He applied it and came back to her. He stroked her from shoulder to thigh and back again, his eyes smoky with lust. 'I think we're going to lose that dinner booking. Do you mind?'

She linked her arms around his neck and smiled. 'Not one little bit.'

As it turned out, they didn't lose the dinner booking, in spite of the mind-blowing sex they'd shared. Louis was nothing if not ruthlessly efficient when it came to giving her pleasure. Her body was still tingling and her lips still swollen from his passionate kisses.

Later that night, Louis sat opposite Ivy at an intimate table in the window of the restaurant a short walk from his apartment. The current of electricity between them seemed to have followed them to the restaurant. Every time she glanced at him, she felt the zap and crackle of energy pass from his gaze to hers. When he reached for her hand across the table, her inner core spasmed with a pleasurable ache.

Ivy picked up her champagne glass and took a sip, conscious of Louis' gaze steadily watching her. She put her glass back down. 'What are you thinking?' It was a bold question to ask but the mood seemed right. Their earlier lovemaking had shifted something in their relationship. Or maybe it was she who had shifted. She felt more confident in her sensuality, more at ease in expressing herself sexually.

His eyes darkened. 'You can't guess?'

A shiver coursed down her spine and sent a soft flicker to her core. 'You're not the easiest person to read but I'm guessing you're thinking about what happens after dinner.'

A slow smile spread across his face and he reached for her hand across the table and held it in his. 'Those diamonds look fabulous on you. The colour reminds me of your cheeks when you blush.'

Ivy touched one of the droplet earrings before placing her hand back in her lap. Her other hand tingled where it was encased in his. 'I'm not sure what Millie is going to say when I come home wearing diamonds from a high-end jeweller. Did I tell you she's a jewellery designer? She lets me wear her stuff for free.'

He pulled his hand away and picked up his glass of champagne, his expression difficult to read. 'They're a birthday gift, that's all.' He took a sip of his drink and placed the glass back on the table with a little thud that seemed to serve as an underline to his statement.

Ivy chewed one side of her mouth. 'Are you cross with me?'

He sighed and gave a forced-looking smile that faded almost as soon as it appeared. 'No. It's just I don't want your friends to get the wrong idea about us. I would have preferred they didn't know about our…arrangement.'

'Well, I get that, but what am I going to say to Ronan or Mum when they see these?' She touched the pendant hanging around her neck.

His mouth tightened. 'I've bought you birthday presents before. What's the big deal?'

'Book and cinema vouchers aren't quite in the same league as diamonds, though, are they?'

Louis picked up his glass and drained it, placing it back down again with a heavy sigh. 'Just for the record, I don't give my ex-lovers diamonds, or any other jewellery when it comes to that.'

'Maybe that's my point.'

A frown settled between his brows. 'And your

point is?' His tone was guarded, and his gaze had 'keep away' written in its smoke and sky hues.

Ivy wished she hadn't started this conversation but felt compelled to continue it regardless. The clock was ticking on 'their arrangement', as he called it. An arrangement that was passionate, exciting and thrilled her senses but was doomed to bring her heartache in the end.

Why hadn't she realised that before now? She was on a road that came to a dead end. It would be crazy to keep driving along it knowing she would never get from Louis what she most wanted. Yes, he'd bought her diamonds and treated her like a princess. He'd made love to her as if she was the only woman in the world he ever wanted to make love to. But he was not willing to open his heart to her.

She took a prickly breath, her heart thumping, her stomach bottoming out. 'My point is I want more than you're offering.'

Not a single muscle moved on his face, but something shifted at the back of his eyes like a furtive shadow at the back of a stage. 'What? Diamonds aren't enough?' His tone had a sarcastic edge.

She sent him a reproving look. 'Louis, I think deep down you want more too, but you're not ready to admit it. You wouldn't have bought me such a beautiful gift if you didn't feel something for me.'

He signalled for the waiter to settle the bill. 'Now is not the time or place to have this conversation.'

'I think it's a perfectly good time,' Ivy said. 'What's the point of us being here together in Paris if we go our separate ways in four days? We have only four days now, Louis. Do you realise how clinical that sounds? You can't put a time limit on your feelings, or at least I can't.' She swallowed and continued, 'I have feelings for you that can't be turned off by a date on the calendar.'

His mouth was so tight, white tips appeared at the corners. 'Look, you're getting confused by the sex. You're new to physical intimacy. People can fancy themselves madly in love with a lover but what they're in love with is the endorphins that good sex sets off. You'll see that I'm right in a few days. Once we stop having sex, you'll—'

'What? Forget how you make me feel? Pretend none of it happened? Come on, Louis, don't you see how much I care about you? It's in every kiss and touch. Every time we make love I give all of myself to you, not just my body, but all of me. I love you.'

He grimaced, as if suffering a deep pain. 'You don't know what you're saying, Ivy. You'll be embarrassed by this in the weeks ahead. I can guarantee it. You're seeing me through oxytocin-tinted glasses—it's the sex hormone that makes people feel bonded to a lover. We have no bond other than friendship. This fling we're having—'

'It's not a fling to me!' Ivy interjected, her heart contracting with anguish at his constant use of that horrible word. 'It's never been a fling or an arrangement. I think on some level I always knew that it could never be that. I think I asked you to help me with my intimacy issues because I loved you. I wouldn't have asked you if I didn't. I see that now. It had to be you because it's always been you I loved.'

'Look—one of the reasons I only have flings is because of this sort of thing happening,' he said. 'I let people down without even trying. I told you from the start what I was prepared to give. It upsets me to see you hurt, knowing I have caused it.' He rubbed a hand over his face and shook his head as if he couldn't believe how he had got himself into this situation. 'I'm sorry, Ivy, but this is all I can give you right now.'

Diamonds. Memories. A clock ticking on their fling. 'It's not enough. And I don't think it's enough for you either. You feel bad about this situation because it clashes with how you think of yourself and the way you really want to be. That's the source of your pain, not the fact you've let me down or any number of other people down. You've let *you* down. The true you.'

The waiter approached with the bill and Ivy was forced to contain her emotions until the transaction was processed. Louis silently led her out of the restaurant, his expression going into lockdown. It wasn't the way she wanted their evening to end but, now she had come to her senses, she had no choice but to see this through. She could not keep driving down a dead end until she crashed into Louis' emotional stop sign.

They walked back to his apartment in silence. His expression might have been closed but Ivy could feel Louis' frustration coming off him in waves. Even the sound of his key stabbing into the lock and the way he opened the door hinted at his brooding tension. He closed the door with a snap and tossed his key onto the hall table with a careless flick of his hand. The key landed into a ceramic bowl with a noisy clatter.

'I told you from the start how uncomfortable I was about this whole plan of yours,' Louis said. 'You have only yourself to blame for how it's turned out now.'

Ivy pressed her lips together, trying to gather her composure. She didn't want to end their fling in a slanging match. But their fling *had* to end. Tonight. Now. Not another day could go past with her continuing to fool herself their relationship would turn into something else. He had made it abundantly, blatantly, brutally clear it wouldn't. 'Louis, this is not easy for me to say, but I want to finish our fling now. It wouldn't be right for me to sleep with you again, not under these terms. I don't want to cheapen what we've shared.'

'I could hardly call what we've shared cheap.' His tone was cruelly sardonic, his glittering gaze cutting as he glanced at the diamonds in her ears and around her neck.

Ivy stiffened as anger spread through her. So, that was the way he wanted to play it, was it? She purposefully removed each earring and placed them in the ceramic bowl with his keys. She placed her hands behind her neck to undo the fastening of the pendant, glaring at him with icy disdain. 'I've decided I prefer book and cinema vouchers after all. Maybe you can find some other fling partner to give these to. I don't want them.'

His top lip curled, and his eyes flashed. 'What? You don't want to take home a souvenir of your first love affair?'

She ground her teeth so hard, she thought she would crack a molar. 'Love affair? On my part, maybe, but not yours. You've hardened your heart out of fear, the same way I avoided intimacy out of fear for all those years. You won't allow yourself to get close to anyone in case they hurt you or make you feel vulnerable. You've got intimacy issues, Louis. You won't ever be happy unless you address them. You're not at heart a playboy. You remind me of Ronan, pretending all those years to be something he's not and could never be. You are a man who wants to love and be loved but you're too frightened to give anyone the power to hurt you.'

Louis threw his head back and gave a cynical laugh that grated on her already shredded nerves. 'Stick with antiques, *ma petite*. You'd make a lousy therapist.' His laughter lines faded and his expression tightened. 'I'm perfectly happy with my playboy lifestyle.'

She raised her chin, giving him a level stare. 'Then you won't mind going back to it sooner rather than later. I'm going home tomorrow morning. There's no point me staying here in Paris with you any longer. Our relationship was always coming to a dead end and I should have seen your emotional stop sign at the end of the road a whole lot earlier. I'll sleep in the spare room tonight.'

'Fine. You do that.' His voice was clipped, his expression tightly drawn. He reached for his keys in the ceramic bowl and added, 'I'm going out. I'll see you in the morning.'

No, you won't, Ivy decided on the spot. *I'll be long gone by then.*

Louis walked several blocks, trying to get his emotions in some sort of working order. *His emotions.* What a joke. He didn't possess the emotions Ivy wanted him to feel. Of course he cared about her— why else had he bought her such an expensive gift for her birthday? Why had he been so reluctant to enter into their fling in the first place?

Hurting her was the last thing he wanted to do.

He should have known it would end this way—with her upset with his lack of commitment. But he couldn't change what was an essential part of his character. He wasn't the marriage and babies type. He could think of nothing more claustrophobic than ending up in a marriage like that of his parents.

His father had promised 'in sickness and health' and got more sickness than health. His mother had promised 'to love and to cherish' and ended up loathing and criticising. Ivy's own parents had done the same, along with numerous others. Love, when and if it even existed in the first place, never lasted. It had never lasted for him. He had occasionally felt flickers of something for the odd partner, and he had definitely felt more than a flicker for Ivy, but it didn't mean it would last the distance.

It would pass. It always did.

And it would again.

CHAPTER TEN

IVY QUICKLY PACKED her things and then called a cab to take her to a hotel closer to the airport. Within the space of minutes, she was out of his apartment and on her way back to her old life. But her life would not be the same as before. She had changed, and those changes had come about through her relationship with Louis. She had seen sex as something to get out of the way, a box to be ticked. But he had shown her how pleasurable sex could be with a partner you trusted. Sex for her was never going to be a simple scratching of an itch, a purely physical response to stimuli. She needed more, she wanted more, she ached for more.

She *deserved* more.

She was not just a body that had needs and desires. She was an adult woman who craved intimacy that went beyond the physical expression of lust. An emotional intimacy. A deep and lasting bond that would only be enhanced by physical passion.

She had hoped Louis felt the same way about her. Hoped and dreamed he would open his heart to her, but where had those hopes taken her?

To a dead end.

It was time to do a U-turn and get on with the rest of her life. Without Louis. Without the love she so desperately craved. Without her happy-ever-after fairy tale.

Louis came back to his apartment an hour or so later and immediately sensed Ivy was gone. The atmosphere was dull, listless, as if the energy had been taken out of the air, leaving it stale and empty. His bedroom door was open, the bed where they had made passionate love only hours ago neatly made, the sheets and covers drawn up, as if to remove any imprint of her having been there. He ruthlessly pulled the covers back off the pillows and picked one up and buried his face in it, breathing in the scent of her fragrance.

Go after her. Bring her back. Don't let her leave like this.

His conscience prodded him from a place deep inside where he never visited. A place where he hid away all the feelings he forbade himself ever to feel. A place that contained a sliver of hope that he could have a different life other than punishing hours of work and transient relationships that left no impression on him other than a vague sense of dissatisfaction. He thought of a life with Ivy—a life where he could be the knight in shining armour she longed for. But how could he guarantee his armour wouldn't lose its shine some day, as his father's had done for his mother? How could he guarantee he wouldn't hurt her or disappoint her the way he'd hurt and disappointed his family?

The only thing he lived for was his work. It was the only thing that satisfied him. It gave him money, loads of money, and numerous accolades that proved his decision to become an architect had been the right decision.

Letting Ivy go was another difficult decision that he knew would prove to be the right one. Four more days in Paris with her might have been the biggest mistake of his life to date.

Yes, it was better that she was gone, even if it felt like hell. It wouldn't feel like this forever.

But, hey, he didn't feel anything forever, right?

This too would pass.

'Hey, why are you back so early?' Millie asked when Ivy came into the flat the following day. 'I thought you were going to be away until—'

'Don't ask.' Ivy slipped her tote bag off her shoulder with a despondent sigh.

'Okay, but judging by the redness of your eyes I'd say you've recently spent a considerable amount of time in tears. Am I right?'

Ivy nodded. 'Yep. I ended things with Louis. I told him I loved him and wanted more than a fling, but of course, he didn't say it back.'

'Oh, honey, I'm so sorry.' Millie enveloped Ivy in a bone-crushing hug. After a moment, she eased back to look at her. 'I was worried from the outset this was going to happen. But are you absolutely sure he doesn't feel the same way about you?'

Ivy slipped out of her friend's embrace. 'I know you did, and I stupidly didn't recognise it until it was already too late. I think I've always been a bit in love with him. And when he bought me the pink diamonds…'

'He bought you pink diamonds?' Millie's eyes were as big as saucers. Satellite-sized saucers.

Ivy shrugged one shoulder. 'He bought them for my birthday, but I mistakenly thought they some-how signified he was falling in love with me. I was wrong. Big time.' Heartbreakingly wrong.

Millie nibbled at one side of her mouth. 'I guess that means he won't be coming to your party, then.' She suddenly clamped her hand over her lips. 'Oops, forget I said that.'

Ivy frowned in puzzlement. 'What party?'

Millie's cheeks were pink, her grey-blue eyes troubled. 'I'm sorry. It was supposed to be a sur-prise. I'm rubbish at keeping a secret. Zoey and I planned to have a party on your birthday, and we sent Louis an invitation last night via email. We told him it was a secret. We thought you'd like him to come.'

'How did you get his email address?'

'Off his website.'

Ivy couldn't think of anything worse than Louis turning up at her birthday party, especially when she had nothing to celebrate other than getting a year older and having her heart broken in the process. 'Cancel it. I don't want a party. I've never felt less like celebrating.'

Millie looked horrified. 'Oh, Ivy, you can't let a milestone like this pass by without some sort of celebration. We've gone to a lot of trouble, and a lot of people will be disappointed if you don't show up. You can still pretend to be surprised. Please don't tell Zoey I let it slip. She'll roast me alive. She's done a lot of the planning and would be so upset if she thought—'

Ivy sighed. 'Okay, let's go ahead with the party.' She just hoped that Louis wouldn't spoil it even further by showing up.

Louis was so distracted by what had happened in Paris that he didn't check his emails until he was on the flight back to London the following afternoon. Which was frankly weird and totally out of character for him. He could normally set a world record for the amount of daily screen time he used. But, no, he had pushed work aside to ruminate over the disaster of the end of his fling with Ivy. An end he'd known was coming from the start but had allowed himself to think wouldn't hurt *him*. How misguided had he been? But he was only feeling this searing pain in his gut because he had disappointed her. It had nothing to do with anything else. What else could it be?

He scrolled through the dozens of emails and saw the invitation to a surprise party for Ivy's thirtieth birthday. He mentally groaned. No way could he show up and cause any more hurt to her. He would ruin the party for her. He would have to stay away and send a present, hoping she wouldn't throw it back in his face.

But not pink diamonds.

Definitely *not* pink diamonds.

A couple of days later, Louis was on his way to work when he got a call from his mother, informing him his father had been rushed to hospital during the night with a heart scare. Louis dropped everything to meet her on the cardiac ward. When he arrived, his father was lying asleep on a bed, hooked up to various monitors, and his mother was sitting white-faced and pinched-looking beside him.

'Oh, Louis, I was so frightened I was going to lose him,' she choked.

Louis went over to her and enveloped her in a hug. He suddenly realised it had been years since he had last hugged his mother. Their usual greetings and farewells were little more than impersonal air-kisses. Not full-on hugs where you could feel the other's heart beating against your own. How had their relationship got so distant? 'I'm here now.' He slowly put her from him but kept hold of her hands. 'How is he?'

She blinked back tears. 'The specialist said it was a mild heart attack. He's booked in for some scans with the possibility of surgery, but we have to wait and see. He's sleeping now. He was awake most of the night complaining of chest pain but he wouldn't let me call an ambulance. He kept saying it was indigestion, but in the end, I rang anyway.'

'Good decision. At least he's safe here now,' Louis said, and released her hand to glance at his sleeping father. That was another sudden realisation—his father was his mother's world. She would be shattered if she lost him. And, when he thought back to the time when she had been in the clinic, his father had been equally distraught at the prospect of losing her. Who could figure out love in all its guises?

'Yes, he's safe.' She gave a little shudder and tried to smile but it didn't quite work. 'I'm sorry for calling you in such a state. I know you're frightfully busy.'

'Not too busy to be here for you when I'm needed.'

Her eyes watered up again. 'Louis, I know your father can be difficult at times, but he's not had it easy. I'm wondering now if the stress of his work has contributed to his heart condition. He never wanted to be an accountant, but he felt pressured by your grandfather. Deep down, I think he's a bit jealous of you—that you had the courage and grit to find your own pathway in life. He's proud of you, in his way. As indeed I am. Your dad is a good man. Oh, I know he finds fault far more than favour, but he's never been unfaithful, in spite of all my mental health struggles. I haven't been the easiest wife to live with, but I love him. He's the only man I've ever loved—apart from you, of course.'

Louis enveloped her in another tight hug. 'Thank you. I love you too.'

A couple of days later, after his conversation with his mother, Louis was working on a new design for a hotel in New York and trying not to think about Ivy. Every hour of the day he tried not to think of how unhappy he had made her, not to mention himself.

But at least he had other things that had gone better for him just lately. His father was back home after having had a stent inserted and was recovering well, even talking of retirement. Louis had seen a remarkable change in how his parents spoke to each other. The health scare had helped each of them realise the deep care and affection they still had for each other. And he liked to think he saw a change in how they spoke to him. Each time he visited, he enveloped both of them in a hug, enjoying their new-found closeness. He had come to understand his father's sacrifice of his own dreams and aspirations, and it humbled Louis to think of how difficult and painful that must have been for him, and why it had impacted his relationship with his only son.

Louis recalled Ivy's comments about him not being true to himself about what he really wanted. He had been true to himself about his desire to pursue architecture. He hadn't let anything or anyone get in the way of his hopes and dreams. But his personal life had suffered. He had fixed things with his parents but his relationship with Ivy was still a sore point. He kept revisiting it, mulling over each moment he'd spent with her, wondering if he could have done anything differently and not ended up with this infernal pain burrowing into his chest. It wasn't indigestion. It wasn't a heart attack…or maybe it was. Not a genuine, medical heart attack, but his heart was definitely hurting in a way it never had before.

But he would have to get over it. Work would have to go back to filling the hole Ivy had left in his life. A hole *he* had foolishly allowed to open.

Louis was thinking about how much he needed a coffee when his office door opened after the briefest of knocks. He looked up to see Natalie, his secretary, who was currently on maternity leave, standing there with a baby strapped to her chest in a sling carrier.

'Hi, Louis. How come no one's manning the desk? Where's the temp—Maureen?'

Louis pushed his computer mouse aside and scowled. 'She called in sick.' He didn't wish ill health on anyone, but he was relieved he didn't have to deal with any more of Maureen's questions about why he'd come home early from Paris.

Natalie's brows rose and she came further into the room, one of her hands carefully cradling her baby's downy head. 'Do you want me to call for a replacement? You look busy as usual, and more than a little frazzled, to be perfectly honest.'

His scowl deepened. 'You're supposed to be on mat leave.'

'And you're supposed to congratulate me on the birth of my baby and gush over him like everyone else does.'

'Didn't you get the flowers and presents I sent you?'

'Yes, they were lovely. You're great at buying presents.'

'Glad somebody thinks so.' His tone was so dry, he could have offered his services as a nappy for the baby. He still had those wretched pink diamonds. He looked at them every day just to remind himself of his foolishness in agreeing to Ivy's plan.

He moved a little closer to Natalie. She could have been carrying a bomb strapped to her chest by the way he was feeling. Babies freaked him out a bit. More than a bit. They were so tiny and needy and…and cute. Yes, heart-squeezing cute, even if he said so himself. 'What's his name?'

'Thomas Charles,' Natalie said, unclipping the carrier, taking the sleeping baby out and handing him to Louis. 'Want to have a cuddle?'

Louis wanted to say no but didn't want to offend her. Mothers had a thing about their babies. His mother had told him recently about her utter devastation as each of her subsequent pregnancies since his birth had failed—how she had loved and grieved for those unborn children, even though she had only been a few weeks along. Somehow, he found himself holding the baby, not as expertly as he would have liked, but the kid didn't seem to mind. Thomas opened his tiny mouth and yawned, and one of his little starfish hands came out. Louis offered his index finger and the baby grasped it. His chest felt as if the baby had grasped onto his heart as well. 'Oh, wow, he's really cute. I can't believe how tiny he is.'

'He didn't feel tiny when I was pushing him out.'

'Spare me the details.' Louis couldn't stop staring at the baby's tiny features and thought about how amazing it must be to see a part of yourself in the next generation. The baby broke wind loudly and Louis quickly passed him back to his mother with a grimace. 'You'd better take him back. This suit is expensive.'

Natalie crooned over the baby as she strapped him back into the sling carrier. 'So, how have you been, Louis? Seen any more of Ellen?'

He stared at her blankly. 'Ellen?'

'Stalker Ellen. Has she been hassling you any more or has she finally got the message?'

Louis raked a hand through his hair, went back behind his desk and sat in his chair with a thump. 'Haven't heard a peep, thank God.' He hadn't thought of anyone but Ivy. She filled his thoughts every hour of the day and most hours of the night.

Natalie studied him for a moment. 'Are you all right? You don't seem yourself at all. You look like you've had no sleep for a week.'

Was he all right? Not really. And, yes, he hadn't slept for a week, and not just because of his dad's health scare. He hadn't been right since Ivy had left him in Paris. But then, maybe he hadn't been right since the first time he'd kissed her. Making love with her had changed him and he couldn't change back to who he had been before. He couldn't slip back into his old life as a carefree, freedom-loving playboy because, damn it, holding his secretary's adorable little baby had shown him a part of himself he had strenuously denied existed until now. He had refused to acknowledge these past few days, even though it was there in how he had come to his parents' aid, supporting them both through a harrowing time.

He was capable of love—more than capable.

He loved Ivy.

How had he not realised until this moment? Why had he shied away from the core of who he was as a person? He adored her. Worshipped her. Missed her so badly it was destroying him day by day.

Louis sprang out of his chair and swept past Natalie. 'Sorry, Nat. I have to go.' He stopped at the door, came back over to her, kissed her on the cheek and dropped a kiss to the baby's head as well. 'Thank you for making me see what a stupid fool I've been.'

Natalie's smile spread over her face and her eyes twinkled. 'Well, look at you. If I'm not very much mistaken, I'd hazard a guess and say Mr Amazing One-Night Stand has fallen for someone and fallen hard. Am I right?'

Louis grinned. 'You're right.' And then he shot out the door.

Ivy was home alone on Friday night watching a box set—story of her life—when the doorbell rang. Millie and Zoey were supposedly both working late, but she knew from Millie it was a ruse—they were doing last-minute party preparations for tomorrow night. She clicked off the TV and tossed the remote back on the sofa. She went to the front door and opened it to see Louis standing there with a huge bunch of pink roses and a box of chocolates. But, sadly, no black velvet jewellery box.

'May I come in? I have something to say to you.' His expression was tightly set and she mentally prepared herself for another argument. Why did he have to come here and rub it in?

She held his gaze, raising her chin a fraction. 'I think you said everything back in Paris.'

He handed her the roses and the box of chocolates, the tension around his mouth loosening. 'Please, Ivy, hear me out. I wish I could rerun that night and do everything differently.'

Ivy wasn't brave enough to pin too many hopes on his coming to see her. It had been a week since she'd left him in Paris. Over a week with not a single word from him. Why should she think anything had changed? She took the roses and chocolates from him and stepped aside to let him in. 'All right. But make it snappy because it's my birthday party tomorrow and I—'

He frowned. 'You know about the party?'

She blew out a breath and closed the door. 'Millie let it slip but I'm pretending I don't know for Zoey's benefit. She's gone to a lot of trouble and I don't want to ruin it for her.'

'I got an invitation, but I wasn't sure if you'd want me there.'

Ivy moved further inside her flat and put the

roses and chocolates on the coffee table. 'I can't imagine how you'd want to be there now.'

'Ivy. Look at me.' His tone had a note of desperation about it, his expression etched in remorse. 'I can't begin to tell you how much I regret how I handled things in Paris. I was a fool to let you go like that. I don't know why it took me all this time to see what has been staring me in the face from the start. You were right when you said I wasn't being true to myself. I wasn't. I was living a lie, denying any feelings in case they made me vulnerable. But, over the last few days, I've come to understand how little I knew myself—the real me. I had stopped listening to my heart for so long, I didn't recognise the signs that were there all along. I love you. I adore you. I can't imagine my life without you in it—not just as a friend but as my lover, my partner. My wife.'

Ivy stared at him, speechless, for long, heart-stopping seconds. Was she hearing him correctly or was her mind and the foolish hopes it contained conjuring up the words she longed to hear from him? 'I don't know what to say...'

He came to her and grasped her by the shoulders, his eyes pleading. 'Say yes, *mon ange*. Say you'll marry me. Say you'll have babies with me and build a life together.'

Ivy's eyes filled with happy tears, joy bursting out of every cell in her body. She threw her arms around him and hugged him close. 'Oh, Louis, you can't imagine how wonderful it is to hear you say those words. I love you so much. I've been so unhappy, so desperately miserable since I left you. I'd given up hope that we could be together.'

He tilted up her face to gaze into her eyes, his face wreathed in a smile. 'I love you to the depth of my being. I can't bear the thought of another day without you by my side. Marry me, *ma chérie*? I need to hear you say yes otherwise I won't believe you're really mine at last.'

Ivy pressed a kiss to his lips. 'Yes, I will marry you. I can think of nothing I'd love more than to be your wife. You've made me so happy I can barely stand it.'

He cradled her cheeks in his hand, his eyes so full of love it made her heart contract. 'I love everything about you. Your goodness and kindness, your ability to always see the good in people instead of focussing on the bad. You have opened my heart like I thought it never could be opened. I feel I can cope with anything with you by my side.'

Ivy stroked his lean jaw. 'I love everything about you too. You're kind and generous and hard-working to a fault. You're everything I've ever dreamed of in a partner. I know we'll be happy together. I will do everything in my power to make you the happiest man on earth.'

'You made me that by saying yes just now.' He reached into his jacket pocket and took out the flat

rectangular jewellery box she'd left behind in Paris.
'I want you to have these. They'll match the pink
diamond I've purchased to go with them. I thought
Millie might like to design our engagement ring.'

Ivy took the velvet box off him and peeped inside to see the pendant, earrings and beside them a
loose pink diamond. 'Oh, Louis, that's so thoughtful of you. She'll be tickled pink. Ha ha.' She closed
the box and put it to one side so she could return to
his warm and loving embrace. Back where she be-
longed. 'But what changed your mind about being
with me?'

'My dad had a heart scare a few days ago. I spent
a fair bit of time sitting with my mother while he
was being attended to in hospital. I came to understand the dynamic between them a little better. They don't always show it but they truly care
about each other. And something you said a while
back really started to resonate with me. You said
at least my father hadn't run off with someone else
but had stayed loyal to my mother. I'd always seen
that he'd stayed out of fear of her trying to take her
life again, but he stayed with her because he loved
her and didn't want to lose her. He'd only suggested
a separation all those years ago because she was so
unhappy after a miscarriage. He thought she might
be better off with someone else. I've been looking at
all the things that were wrong in their relationship
instead of all the things that are right.'

'Oh, I'm so glad you understand them both a little better. Do you think I can meet them some time? I'd really love to.'

He grinned. 'Of course. I can't wait to show off my beautiful fiancée.' He pressed another kiss to her lips. 'I don't want a long engagement. I want to be married to you as soon as possible. And let's not leave it too long before we start on making a baby.'

Ivy smiled up at him. 'You really mean it? You want to have babies with me?'

He kissed her again. 'Yes. A baby or two, and we'll get a dog too. And I'm going to make your boss an offer on his business. I think you'd be great at running your own antiques business. Or would that be too much?'

Ivy wrapped her arms tightly around his waist, leant her head on his chest and sighed with pure joy. 'That would be perfect.'

EPILOGUE

LOUIS DIDN'T NEED to drink champagne at Ivy's birthday party the following night to feel tipsy. He was drunk on the sight of her dressed in a scarlet velvet dress that clung lovingly to every sweet curve of her body. She was wearing the earrings and pendant he'd given her, and her friend Millie was already working on a design for the engagement ring.

Ivy had done a brilliant job of acting surprised when she'd come into the venue where the party was being held, but ended up being completely surprised by the presence of her brother and father. Louis had taken upon himself to meet with Keith Kennedy that morning and insist he not spoil Ivy's birthday, because Millie had let slip to him in a follow-up email that Ronan and his partner Ricky were flying all the way from Australia to attend. Fortunately, Keith had had the grace and maturity to accept he was wrong and came to the party with an apology in hand. Of course, there was more work to do on Keith's relationship with his son, but these things took time.

Louis had his own family relationships to continue to work on. He could never thank Ivy enough for helping him to see how he'd been far too critical of his parents, viewing their relationship too negatively without seeing the positives. And there were so many positives now his focus had changed. His father had never had an affair…he had never walked out on his wife or son. His father had put all his own dreams and aspirations to one side so he could carry on his own father's business. That was a sacrifice that took enormous courage and commitment. His mother had suffered great sadness and Louis hadn't fully understood how it had impacted her mental health. But he was hoping the birth of grandchildren one day in the future would help his mother continue on her journey to a happier, more positive state of mind.

Ivy moved away from greeting one of the guests and came back to Louis. 'Darling, this is the best party I've ever had. I don't think I've ever been happier than at this very moment. I love you.'

He slipped his arms around her and planted a kiss on her lips. *'Je t'aime, mon ange.* I am happy too. More than I can say. More than I thought possible.'

And he would spend the rest of his life being thankful for his sweet, adorable Ivy.

* * * * *

#3853 THEIR IMPOSSIBLE DESERT MATCH
by Clare Connelly

A chance encounter between Princess Johara and a mystery lover was the perfect night. Until she discovers the man was her family's bitter enemy! Now Johara must travel to Sheikh Amir's desert palace to broker peace...and try to resist their forbidden temptation!

#3854 STEALING THE PROMISED PRINCESS
The Kings of California
by Millie Adams

Prince Javier de la Cruz's goal was simple. Tell heiress Violet King she's promised in marriage to his brother. His first problem? She refuses. His second problem? Their instant, unwelcome and completely forbidden chemistry!

#3855 HOUSEKEEPER IN THE HEADLINES
by Chantelle Shaw

Betsy Miller was ready to raise her son alone after tennis legend Carlos Segarra dismissed their night of passion. Now that the headlines have exposed their child, Carlos is back and everyone's waiting to see what he'll do next...

#3856 ONE SCANDALOUS CHRISTMAS EVE
The Acostas!
by Susan Stephens

Smoldering Dante Acosta has got to be physiotherapist Jess's sexiest client yet. Even injured, the playboy polo champion exudes a raw power that makes Jess giddy...but can she depend on him fighting for their chemistry this Christmas?

HPCNMRB0920

"Your Majesty. Really." Calista moistened her lips and
he found himself drawn to that, too. What was the matter
with him? "You can't possibly think that we would suit
for anything more than a temporary arrangement to
appease my father's worst impulses."

"I need to marry, Lady Calista. I need to produce
heirs, and quickly, to prove to my people the kingdom
is at last in safe hands. There will be no divorce." Orion
smiled more than he should have, perhaps, when she
looked stricken. "We are stuck. In each other's pockets,
it seems."

She blanched at that, but he had no pity for her. Or
nothing so simple as pity, anyway.

He moved toward her, taking stock of the way she
lifted her head too quickly—very much as if she was
beating back the urge to leap backward. To scramble
away from him, as if he was some kind of predator.

The truth was, something in him roared its approval at that notion. He, who had always prided himself on how civilized he was, did not dislike the idea that here, with her, he was as much a man as any other.

Surely that had to be a good sign for their marriage.

Whether it was or wasn't, he stopped when he reached her. Then he stood before her and took her hand in his.

And the contact, skin on skin, floored him.

It was so...*tactile*.

It made him remember the images that had been dancing in his head ever since he'd brought up sex in her presence. It made him imagine it all in intricate detail.

It made him hard and needy, but better yet, it made her tremble.

Very solemnly, he took the ring—the glorious ring that in many ways was Idylla's standard to wave proudly before the world—and slid it onto one of her slender fingers.

And because he was a gentleman and a king, did not point out that she was shaking while he did it.

"And now," he said, in a low voice that should have been smooth, or less harshly possessive, but wasn't, "you are truly my betrothed. The woman who will be my bride. My queen. Your name will be bound to mine for eternity."

Don't miss
Christmas in the King's Bed.

Available October 2020 wherever
Harlequin Presents books and ebooks are sold.

Harlequin.com

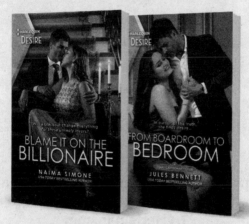

Love Harlequin romance?

DISCOVER.

Be the first to find out about promotions, news and exclusive content!

Facebook.com/HarlequinBooks

Twitter.com/HarlequinBooks

Instagram.com/HarlequinBooks

Pinterest.com/HarlequinBooks

ReaderService.com

EXPLORE.

Sign up for the Harlequin e-newsletter and download a free book from any series at
TryHarlequin.com

CONNECT.

Join our Harlequin community to share your thoughts and connect with other romance readers!
Facebook.com/groups/HarlequinConnection

HSOCIAL2020